MARY
AND HER
SEVEN
DEVILS

MARY AND HER SEVEN DEVILS

PETER MORRIS

BROWN
DOG
BOOKS

Published under licence by Brown Dog Books and
The Self-Publishing Partnership Ltd., 10b Greenway Farm,
Bath Road, Wick, nr. Bath, BS30 5RL

www.selfpublishingpartnership.co.uk

ISBN printed book: 978-1-83952-605-3
ISBN e-book: 978-1-83952-606-0

Cover design by Kevin Rylands
Internal design by Andrew Easton

Front cover picture: *Saint Francis and the Angel* by Orazio
Gentileschi, circa 1607.
La Galleria Nazionale d'Arte Antica, Rome.

Printed and bound in the UK

This book is printed on FSC® certified paper

MIX
Paper | Supporting
responsible forestry
FSC® C013604

To Susan Hubbard
my eternally beloved

DISCLAIMER.

The unscrupulous social work staff depicted in this
story do not relate in any way or to anyone employed
at any time in the Tyneside or North-Eastern
areas of England.

CHAPTER ONE

I am Mary Fleet and this is the story of my quest for freedom, of my search for my *true* self.

The spark was a failed pancake recipe. I had included an over-ripe banana with the result that the batter mix broke up in the pan.

After my frivolous apology, Daddy, eating his pile of fragments with treacle drizzled on top, made some formulaic remark about teenage girls.

I was fourteen and resolved – on the spot – to break out of this don't-say-boo-to-a-goose Kindergarten.

My father – fond of this cute rosy-cheeked rag-doll – tried to dissuade me, but his efforts – though eloquent – were ineffective.

Having realised that much in life is crooked or not what it pretends to be, I wished to reshape my *persona* to co-exist with these shifting sands, yet without becoming a dud or subtracting from my own delightful whims or magic.

Over a milk-shake, I told my friend Josh how Daddy so often blocked any exuberance or caprice.

Josh rocked his head. 'You and he are quite alike.'

'What?' I rasped. 'What a ridiculous load of bull-shit!'

'You're both quite serious?'

'What?!'

He smiled and shrugged. 'Well your mouths have the same shape.'

'Well what comes out of them is chalk and cheese,' I frothed.

We both sucked on our straws.

'You're designed to be an angel Mary, not a demon.'

'I'm still an apprentice ... testing the waters.'

'Anyway, tread warily ... the Yellow Brick Road can end up in Oz where everything's a sham.'

Josh could be amazingly stubborn. 'Yet so can the rose-tinted ... or any other fantasy or humbug. Scrooge in *A Christmas Carol*, ends up saying, "If only ... "' I countered.

He half-conceded. 'We each have to find our own character ... but don't end up like Alex. She treats her parents terribly. Janice calls her "the cheese-grater".'

'I swear not to become a sour hag.' I slurped the last of my milk-shake. 'Daddy's curbs though need to be side-stepped.'

'Suggest he talks to a psychotherapist?'

'One with lots of spare time.'

*   *   *   *

My father, the Reverend William Arthur Fleet, was the priest in a sleepy country parish in Devon.

The new church organist had too much to say, the crucifer was manipulative, the sexton an endless source of negativity and the bell captain too bossy.

He seemed like a mouse surrounded by squabbling cats, who if they came together, might eat him.

I told him it was time for a tiger hunt, it being the prerogative of daughters to try to stiffen morale when the going is tough.

'There are two ways of solving this, Mary,' he explained, 'head on or tunnelling and mining.'

'But the tunnel isn't advancing?'

'Chess grand masters often retreat. To a beginner this looks like poor tactics ... ground is lost, position sacrificed, but then ... *zap!*'

I huffed softly.

Three of us had formed a pop group, *The Orgasmic Spasms*. Nigel on the keyboard played well enough, Emily the flautist was definitely under par and my voice, high-pitched yet a trifle shrill.

With bags of ill-judged confidence and a bouncy tuneful song called *Angel Aura*, we sang at a local concert. I had a frog in my throat and Emily was worse than usual. Everyone smiled and clapped, though for the wrong reasons.

'Still,' said Nigel, 'at least we were better than that other bunch with their melancholic shite.'

At the buffet, I encountered the organist, where I sustained a *détente cordiale* during his none-too-deft sarcasm over my red blue and mauve finger-nails, but snapped when he referred to Emily as 'that grade-one flautist'.

'What about the tuneless rubbish you play by Herbert Howls?'

'Hummable themes are not the sole measure of musical art, Mary.'

'In noble courts stringed instruments give gladness,' I quoted the psalm. 'Not some awful racket.'

'I had you marked down as a rather sweet lass?'

'Lass' sounded like some country girl picking cider apples.

I told him that his organ playing was brash, that he was too big for his boots, that if the choir expanded any more the congregation would be squeezed onto the back pew and that the tail – which was him – was wagging the dog.

Next day he popped a note through our letter-box offering his resignation.

Even Mummy said, 'Well for heaven's sake dear, seize the chance.'

Father beamed like a painted seraph. 'So, my strategy is vindicated?'

The sloth is the living proof that Darwin was up a gum tree.

*   *   *   *

In 2014, as I rocked on the swing under our apple-tree, Daddy – chewing a pencil in a deck-chair nearby – tried to draft a sermon.

Sunday's gospel story told of Mary of Magdala, whom Jesus had cured of seven devils. She may have been a prostitute at the court of Herod Antipas; the jar of perfume with which she had washed the Lord's feet, a gift from a rich lover.

'Is there an analogy there with Snow White and the Seven Dwarfs?'

No reply.

'So what *were* her sins?' I queried. 'Eating pork chops?'

This flippancy too was ignored.

Undeterred, I suggested, 'Throwing a terracotta pot at the village rabbi? Exercising nude in the gymnasium with ... ?'

'I am fed up,' he broke in, 'with sermons. In future, I shall simply underscore one or two of the simpler themes from the set reading.'

'Is that sufficient?'

'Our parishioners Mary, are *not* the brightest.'

Next day, unexpectedly, the bishop came and sat at the back of the church.

Daddy, wrong-footed, stated he had taken a vow; instead of homilies he would allow the Holy Spirit to speak boldly and directly through him.

His discourse, disjointed and peppered with tangled ambiguities, could have been written by a dyslexic in the G stream of the local comprehensive. Alternatively, it was one of those do-it-yourself jokes, where you have to unscramble the speaker's ideas to find the punch line.

Back at the rectory I answered the telephone. It was the Bishop, the Right Reverend Hugh Bontoft.

'He is not come home yet, Your Grace.'

'Then could you please tell him that he is released from his vow?'

*   *   *   *

In my last two years at school, I balanced being an affectionate daughter with defending my patch from Daddy's biased – if sub-textual – censure. I sought the garlands of enthusiasm and happiness, despite any peccadilloes this incurred or its sporadic infringement of my faith in God.

I cringed when Daddy greeted my friends with, 'Hullo girly-whirlies' or when dropping me off to go on trips, his fond farewells were of the overly visible variety.

His inability to detect the ebbs and flows of modern society, left him like an outmoded psychiatrist, who, unable to grasp his patient's fantasies and hang-ups, just doodles quaint figures on his note-pad.

Mary of Magdala's life embodied hints of the epicurean. She seemed spirited; blowing the dust off the old rabbis. I saw her carousing with a young Parthian envoy and extracting secrets from him whilst canoodling on an aloe-and-cassia-sprinkled rug. Spying – the second oldest profession in the world – Mary had possibly combined with the first?

Then university beckoned. Ecstasy. Hats in the air.

My last exams were in French, Italian and ancient history and by reading general arts, I thought to learn some modern Greek and perhaps Arabic, with the vague notion of becoming a travel rep in either Greece or Morocco.

'Teaching is not highly rated today,' said my father, 'but it is giving service to others.'

I gave him a cheesy grin.

CHAPTER TWO

Newcastle University arose like a Phoenix.

In September 2016 Daddy took me up with all my stuff and – delighted by this release from his inelastic 'genius' – I gave him a big hug and a kiss as he left.

He seemed reluctant to go. 'On that Mary Queen of Scots coin, *Ecce ancilla Domini* is what Mary says to Gabriel in Luke; "Behold the handmaid of the Lord".'

I gave him another big kiss and waved him off.

By contrast, outside my upstairs flat in Otterburn Terrace in Jesmond, the water pipes were being replaced in the street by more practically minded labourers, who spent a lot of time in their tin hut, studying the layout.

Next morning, after enrolling, I drifted out into the quad where a number of student societies had set up stalls. Many of these were campaigning against the injustices in society; exposing the damage being inflicted on us by industry, by greed or by sword-rattling imperialists.

The prophet Jeremiah had told the dwellers in Jerusalem that they were wicked and that disaster would befall them. They did not like what he said, so they threw him down a well, piled stones on him and left him for dead. He was though, not dead. Then – as he had foretold – the Babylonians arrived, destroyed the city and took everyone off into captivity.

What clubs might my first-century Mary join?

Perhaps 'The Bacchantes' or the 'Protect unborn Piglets Society,' but there did not seem to be either of those. One existed for raiding farms which bred research animals, but spattered with mud and urine from loosed apes, you might not look so good at the party afterwards?

Yet the gospels do not paint Mary as a stroppy rebel, so perhaps 'The *Tepidarium* Belles'? And after a dip be rubbed with oil, scraped with a strigil and pummelled by some muscle-bound Cypriot? Hmm. It sounded good.

My flat-mate in this split Victorian terrace-house was called Sophie Hughes. She came from Harlech on Cardigan Bay and although also recognising that much was wrong with the world, wanted not to protest – for she believed in peace – but to make sure that she herself lived a pure life. She went round the flat in bare feet, was keen on pumpkin seeds and carrot juice and abstained from beef, because cows apparently produce methane which is destroying the planet. My microwave pasta-bake she explained was eighty per cent flavouring.

She stuck up a poster titled 'Desiderata'. It spoke of 'going quietly amid the noise and haste' and to 'believe in God, whatever you conceive Him to be'. It said at the bottom that it had been found in Saint Paul's church in Baltimore and dated 1770, yet its style and lexicography did not seem to fit that era.

She asked if I would like to go with her to a party in the Politics Department?

She spent a lot of time fixing her hair into some sort of bouffant *coiffure*, then dressed in a black leather mini-skirt and a frilly low-cut white blouse, before dabbing on an abundance of purply-coloured make-ups. I felt a bit dowdy in my cotton skirt and chequered blouse.

We arrived in a large sterile low-ceilinged room with plastic chairs, fluorescent lighting and notice-boards full of crap, but wine was being dispensed both into cups and onto the floor and some indifferent sausage rolls and crisps had been dumped on a table, still in their supermarket wrappers ... Sorry, am I showing here what a snob I have been in the past?

Anyhow, everyone smiled and seemed happy until some girl's boyfriend – who was reading engineering – upset the congenial and thought-provoking exchanges.

This total idiot said that we were all advertising our fake morals to make ourselves look good in front of others. He compared us to the Pharisees in the New Testament who stood on street-corners saying their prayers publicly in order to win the award of others; to look pious.

Well some eff-words certainly flowed. Was this stupid half-wit totally blind to what was going on around us? Had he just mindlessly swallowed the devious lies of those pro-American dissemblers with their hidden short-sighted motives of gain? Was life just about the vulgar amassing of wealth? 'You're utterly bamboozled, man,' said a shaggy Ethiopian. 'We need change. We need equality.'

'Never mind depth,' some petite lass taunted him. 'Just live with your empty superficiality.'

A junior lecturer with a deformed leg, one Céline Seddon, sighed and whispered that she and most of the staff in their discipline were careful to screen out such potential trouble-makers at interview.

Professor Jones, who looked close to retirement

and was a touch aristocratic, spoke mostly about his nineteen-twenties Hornby 'O' gauge toy railway. Was it Nero who played the lyre whilst Rome burnt?

A lanky French girl said she was studying icebergs. They were just *so* interesting.

Yet did Mary of Magdala fit this protest-robot monologue-chanting stuff? She came of lowly stock and had dwelt amidst conflict and division, yet contrariwise had herself been bewitching it seemed, enjoying intimacies with the Herodian dynasty's upper circles. I saw her as a touch coy, blasé or droll. She must also have been outstandingly pretty.

I do not like alcohol and so the next day, fully sober, went out, bought all my course books and set to, to study Modern Greek Level 1, Swedish Level 1 and Archaeology Level 1. I had chosen the latter as I thought it might lead to a summer field-trip in some interesting foreign country, like Syria say or the Yemen?

For two weeks I worked pretty solidly, making an effort to get to grips with this stuff. Swedish – oscillating up and down by a musical fourth – had a possible similarity with classical Greek, where the 'long' syllables might have also been raised in pitch, as opposed to being accented.

But, after two weeks, with still no boyfriend and social interaction limited to just the odd cup of coffee with some of my class-mates, I was tempted when Sophie mentioned a plan to sabotage a coal train.

Someone in the 'Climate Club' knew the details of its route and its timings on the way to some disgusting power station which was belching out carbon monoxide ... or was it dioxide? Anyway, something terribly harmful.

Sophie, five foot seven and with her light-brown hair, seemed quite wound-up. She had a dull flare across her left cheek. It seemed that her new boyfriend had said to her that whilst criticising these power stations, she always left lights on everywhere. She had told him to eff-off and thrown some tea at him, whereupon he had belted her across the face and kicked her out.

Still, it sounded like an exciting adventure and a much needed break from syntax and oblique declensions.

'What should we wear?' I asked her. 'Not leather mini-skirts, I take it?'

'Why not?' she asked with a grin.

'Well ... you might snag your tights for a start.'

CHAPTER THREE

Gold, almug wood and peacocks were ferried from Ophir for Herod's exotic court.

Yet in first-century Judaea also, the Zealots sought to ambush their Graeco-Roman conquerors, whilst the sicarii – with their secreted curved knives – mingled with the crowd and stabbed any apostate Jew who had engaged in pagan or Hellenistic rites.

Their wives and daughters stayed at home, stirring the couscous.

Happily though, we girls are now free to speak and to ride into battle.

It was an unusually cold October evening. I wore walking boots, thick socks and a woollen skirt, but only a thin summer anorak.

Sophie asked, 'Will you be warm enough?'

I looked at her. 'You sound like my mother.'

Ten of us knelt in the long grass and cow-parsley on the embankment. Gavin had brought some heavy-duty wire-cutters and cut enough strands of barbed wire to let us onto the tracks. The train though was late. Were those troublesome drivers on strike again? The twilight faded, a quarter moon rose, an owl hooted mockingly and nettles stung my legs.

An engine rumbled past hauling a string of empty wagons away from the power station. I had not realised how big railway wagons were. It would not be easy climbing onto them.

It started to rain. Sophie had dressed more sensibly;

ex-marine combat trousers, two jumpers and a cagoule.

After two hours of shivering, we gave up. The last bus had gone, so we had to walk six miles back into town.

Some of us went into a petrol station to buy some chocolate or a drink. Two cars were filling up in the forecourt and to one side a girl sat astride a motorbike. We must have looked pretty odd, carrying shovels at that hour.

'Do you think the fuzz have been tipped off?' queried George.

The next day, as I sat sipping hot lemon juice, the door-bell rang and I went downstairs.

It was Adrian, one of the boys from next door. 'Is Sophie in?'

'She's in the shower.'

'We're having a party on Saturday, but ... ' he stepped back and eye-balled me approvingly, 'you're invited too.'

I gave a wry 'flattery-will-get-you-everywhere' grin, but thanked him.

In the kitchen nook Sophie made tea.

As I sneezed, she said, 'I don't feel too good either. I've a bit of a discharge. I'm off to see the doc in half an hour.'

I was surprised she had told me this.

'So stupid to have been enthralled by that geo-physicist numbskull.'

When alone, I viewed myself in the long oval mirror.

I was taller and probably more attractive than Sophie, who though in fairness had a homely and bonny warmth about her and a slight action-girl aura, unlike many listless or timid students. She could too be quite a live-wire when she put her mind to it. My face was perhaps more delicate with its sharper features and arched brows? I stood back and oscillated my hips. I simply needed to make more effort with my hair and clothes. My present shabbiness stemmed in part from trying to irritate my parents.

Saturday night came. Sophie and I went round, each with a bottle of *rosé*.

Lilac and violet lights flashed.

'The doctor says I'm on the mend, but he had the nerve to ask, "How's your sex life?" I nearly said, "Excellent thanks. How's yours?"'

A bozo with halitosis and boils sized me up.

'Lush.'

'Sorry?'

'What a smooth, slender, hour-glass figure?' he mused. 'What's far rarer though is a stunning face.' He gave a deep sigh. 'And yours could launch those thousand ships.'

I tilted my eyebrows critically. 'Only a thousand?' I sipped my grapefruit juice to see if this delightful commentary would continue.

'So, why are you not an actress or a model?'

I looked unsure.

'Because you lack someone who can pull strings.'

'So are you offering me a *rôle* in your next high-budget film?'

'Shall we go to my flat and discuss the details?'

I demurred. 'It would be rude to leave so early.'

He smiled wanly, as if to say, 'Worth a shot.'

Kevin and Yvonne seemed to be joined at the hip. Threadbare clichés alternated with approval-seeking smiles.

Yvonne felt her pocket. 'Where's my note-book?' She glanced around the floor.

Tom, a junior lecturer, whispered, 'Jane Austen judges whether someone is grown up, by whether they know their own mind.'

'Oh?'

'Or if they're just repeating stuff?'

'Is there some bird – a kookaburra is it – which can imitate all sorts of sounds ... even chain-saws?'

The music, being at a low level, meant we could talk instead of simply exchanging stares; flirtatious, nonchalant or discouraging, as the inclination took you.

The lads here – Adrian, Rob and Julian – read physics, yet only seemed to talk about ancient battlefields or scuba-diving.

I asked Adrian about the heavy-metals killing the fish in the Tyne and the heat-trapping toxic gases polluting the er ... icosi-sphere?

'Or the I-don't-know-o-sphere?' He gave me a playful peck on the cheek.

I blushed in the gloom.

'Mary, forget that bollocks. What counts is fizz, sagas, fair maidens ... '

A home-daubed mural on the wall showed a sexy blonde with a speech-balloon which read, 'And this morning I feel *so* beautiful.'

'Did you paint that?' I grinned.

'Me?' he protested, then cackled.

Julian said, 'Geese on the ground are a gaggle, in the air a skein.'

'Two collective nouns for one species?'

Sophie, who had recoalesced with us, described the egrets wading on the shore-line near Aberaeron, where she had spent a year before university working in a Forestry Commission office.

Someone called, 'Yvonne? Is this your note-book?'

She wandered over.

'Some wine's been spilt on it ... smudging this Yom Kippur blurb ... and this cod's head image?'

'Yes, it is mine. No, that's a footprint. Thanks Erica.'

'Yom Kippur?' said some girl. 'The day when Jews can't eat kippers.' She seemed to have her hands up her back, unhooking her bra.

Tom reappeared. 'I hear you're reading Swedish?'

'Yes.'

'I teach Old Icelandic ... and modern.'

'Swedish has undergone more change?'

'Yes. Industry, the theatre, Nobel and his dynamite ... all required a broader linguistic palette.'

'I prefer their films,' mused Julian. 'After some token scything of hay, the real action's up in the hay-loft.'

We all tittered softly. 'An about-turn in their sexual attitudes in the fifties.'

'Or just a coming to the surface?'

In a larger circle, I listened to some fairly near-the-bone banter and thought how different it was from the stilted chaff over tea and buns in the parish hall back at Sloe Buxcomb. There we all hid much of what we thought, a *sine qua non* if we were to maintain smooth social cohesion. At university – by contrast – you were free to show off, tease or make mistakes.

As I left at eleven o'clock, Tom left too.

In the little weed-filled front garden, he asked, 'Mary, would you like to come back for coffee?'

I found myself staring quizzically into his slightly globulous eyes and saying, 'All right.'

In retrospect, I am unsure why I accepted. I had no strong feelings for him nor am I one of those girls who just wants to advertise that she can lasso a man.

In his sub-warden's flat in Easton Hall, I sat on the sofa and thumbed a book of Norwegian regional costumes until he brought in the coffee, some savoury biscuits and various cheeses.

I had only once been properly kissed. That was by Andy Slade behind our village pub. He had been good, but on reflection too pushy, too intense, too fast.

I sipped my coffee and waited.

Tom Horrocks was thin, shy, late twenties and from Lancaster.

'As we touched on earlier, Swedes were a dour, practical folk who cast off Puritanism almost overnight ... or so it seems?'

I wondered, 'Are you a man or a mouse?'

Dipping his toe in the water, he put an arm round my shoulders and we kissed in a rather clumsy and experimental way.

I was still a virgin and so hoped that my first encounter – when it happened – would be with someone similarly inexperienced. Tom though did not try and anyway, I would never allow that at a first meeting.

He mentioned Sweden's near monopoly of iron smelting, before Abraham Darby discovered how to use coke instead of charcoal.

'I'm sure that's *very* interesting,' I said. 'Who's that in the picture?'

'Oh ... my sister. Hollie.'

She wore a startling, shiny, copper-effect vinyl dress.

'She's an *Ultra-Girl* fan club member.'

'Oh.'

'It's a cult film. They hold events and dress up.'

I finished my cheese, allowed him to stroke my hair a little, smiled and then stood up to take my leave.

He saw me home.

Sophie had stayed at the party until one-thirty, eaten – for a lark – a tiny finger of cannabis cake and then wandered into the road and almost under a taxi. In the flat she spoke of a red sock which had climbed into a wash-tub and of a bone-headed helix of orange peel, but the flagship of these rhapsodies were her colourful knights with their three-foot penises.

I steered her into the bathroom to have a wee, then into her own room, where I put her in bed and turned out the light.

Curiously the motorbike at the petrol station flashed into my mind. The girl, stoical and slim, had worn a one-piece black leather motorcycle suit and boots. She had sat toying with her helmet and gloves, her demeanour bright yet calm and suddenly I knew that she had been a plain clothes police officer.

Next day Sophie swore, 'Never, never again.'

Tom and I took protracted walks – usually on

Saturdays – and though we were not especially close, we chatted easily enough about a broad swathe of topics and usually stopped for a light meal somewhere.

I and my school friend Ruth had once debated 'love' and acknowledged that it was unique and came from God. A year later though, she capitulated. 'You grow tired of waiting. You *so* want something to happen.'

For my eighteenth birthday, Tom took me to a country-house-style restaurant at a golf club up in Northumberland.

I tried oysters for the first time, which were slimy and tasted solely of salt water. The halibut, spinach and crusty rolls with butter were excellent, the coffee and cake – called 'two shots in the bunker' – good, but the company insipid. Tom discussed at insufferable length which stuffed tomato filling to choose for his mother's sixtieth birthday party. He asked the young waitress about her 'interesting' tattoos, whilst the couple at the next table discussed from which side of the bush the grapes used to make their wine had been picked. I nearly threw a tantrum and walked out.

My school nickname had been 'Muff', based on the initials of my name – Mary Una Fleet – with the 'f' doubled. I began to feel more miffed than muffed. Mary of Magdala sought out things more heroic, more colourful than this in the temples and palaces of Galilee.

Tom's present had been a colour-illustrated book on women's football. Since I have absolutely zero interest in sport, how much thought had gone into that?

Walking home one evening, I gazed up at the bluish-white stars, slowly rotating in those cold and far-off heavens. As they twinkled, I heard a voice. 'Mary, keep seeing Tom. It's safer for you at present.'

We all play board games with our lives and it is not wholly bad. Too much truth can be difficult. Make-believe gold ingots or paste blue sapphires are nice friendly substitutes for darker realities. We use one another and mimic others' delusions and it gives us a temporary happiness; a step we hope on the path to a higher wisdom.

Sophie and I rubbed along well enough. We trusted one another and quite often she asked about my Greek studies.

Academically all she did was to write an occasional essay. She rarely attended lectures, seldom opened a book and yet said they had her pencilled in for a two-one. Sometimes at the weekend, she drove a mini-bus in South Shields, unless there was a party, which of course took precedence.

Apart from the medics downstairs, I seemed to be the only one studying hard, though luckily I did like my subjects.

Then before Christmas, I made fun of someone, which was very wrong of me.

We had been given some tickets for a reception in the Laing Art Gallery in the city centre and decided that we should dress more stylishly than usual.

Sophie's cheeks were quite pitted, a result of her using too much make-up. I suggested she stop using the thick stuff, but she said that now she needed it to hide the pitting.

'That will only make it worse.'

From pots of blues and reds and with a casual artless humour, she dabbed blotches of deep pink onto my cheeks.

I gave a smile and wiped them off. 'I don't wish to look like a geisha puppet from the twenties.'

As I sat facing the mirror, she leant a forearm on my shoulder. 'Odd you should say that?'

I gave a puzzled shake of the head.

'I'm going to Tokyo for Christmas.'

'Gosh?'

'My sister Megan's won a magazine prize. Two weeks.'

Deciding that I could not say 'Gosh' a second time, I said, 'How wonderful,' then, 'Do the Japanese celebrate Christmas?'

'It's called "The Festival of the Green Chrysanthemum".'

'Well, you'll have no trouble with the jet-lag.'

'What?'

'You're seldom up before noon.'

She hammered me playfully on the head and we set off.

In the stone-arched foyer four elegant and well-to-do girls were being approached by prosperous-looking fellows in dinner jackets and bow-ties. Their shrill laughter conveyed a sense of 'We're eager, come take us,' whilst the men's throaty bass compliments seemed to echo back, 'We know. We're coming.'

Sophie went to talk to someone called Duncan and so – with a glass of fizzy water – I wandered off round the preview of this forthcoming exhibition.

A pale fellow came up to me wearing a grey smock, a belted, sleeveless, reversed-sheep-skin jerkin and a beret.

'What does "post-modernism" mean,' I asked. 'Do you have to be clairvoyant?'

He adjusted his pose. 'No. "Modernism" was a new technique, but for subject matter it still used traditional themes. "Post-modernism" is a style unshackled from all historical content or obsolete faiths or tenets.'

I sensed that he was lonely, a little pretentious and that he lusted for me. Rather wickedly, I chose to mislead him.

'So, a blank canvas?'

'Sort of.'

It had to be based on something, surely? 'Sort of?'

'Yes. It's quite esoteric ... not easy to explain.'

He said he had studied in Lucca and that he did volunteer work for the charity 'Relief in Africa'.

We were stood in front of a painting whose swirls of orange and yellow appeared entirely abstract.

He read the label. 'This represents two aikido experts fighting.'

I eyed the signature. 'By Deborah Samson. A Philistine?' He looked puzzled, so I emphasised, 'Samson?'

He leered none too discreetly at my lower parts.

I invoked a touch of that shy aura which my father had once nurtured in me. Recalling Delilah's talents in this field, I rubbed his ego with a coy smile.

Thinking he had blurred my radar or outwitted my cavalry, he asked me back to his 'studio'.

I snubbed him with a faint snort and danced off to join Sophie.

A Lebanese patron stood boasting of his business successes.

'What was his bank manager's name?' someone whispered with dry irony.

Back in Jesmond, Sophie heated some Bakewell tart and custard. Some hot jam stuck to my palate and burnt it, like the napalm used in Vietnam.

I told her of my 'de-escalation' of the lecherous art student. 'I ran some simple Italian past him, which he didn't understand.'

She stayed silent.

'Yet I daresay we can all end up with egg on our faces ... or worse?'

She said flatly, 'Mary, that was not worthy of you.'

Sophie could at times be quite severe. I looked at her and felt humbled, even ashamed.

'It sounds pitiful.'

'Yes, I know.' I put my face into my hands. 'I'm sorry.'

She gazed at me thoughtfully. 'Why did you do it? I'll tell you. Because you're not exactly over the moon about Tom.'

I sighed softly.

O Lord, if only my ways were made straight?

Changing subject, she harangued me about her last essay. It had been marked not by Professor Jones, but by that stuck-up, chip-on-her-shoulder Doctor Seddon. A C treble-minus really was bad. 'And it's the best thing I've written yet. That damn witch.'

I commiserated. 'Doesn't she like you?'

Sophie was speechless.

'In something like maths, you couldn't do that. An answer's either right or it's not.'

'They say that when she came here two years ago,

on day one the Professor called her "My dear," to which she retorted, "Don't patronise me."'

'Send her a Christmas card with demonic symbols added in invisible ink?'

We had our oven-ready Christmas lunch the next day.

Sara from my Swedish set came. She had blown most of her term's allowance on clothes in the first week and so survived to an extent on charity.

Sibylle – the German medical student downstairs – was alone as her flat-mates had gone down, so we invited her up.

Sophie floated her C treble-minus essay thorn. 'I just said that prejudice and intolerance do a lot to define what we are and if you had none, would you be an empty shell, a nonentity?'

Sibylle sipped her wine. 'I upset the dermatology professor ... so he gave me an E.'

'Trod on his tootsies?'

'Tootsies?' She looked bemused.

'Toes. Baby language.'

We talked of baby words – 'chuckie-egg' and such – and Sara said her flat-mate who did Portuguese, though she had learnt all sorts of modern jargon, had not known the word for 'goose'.

Being Christmas, even I had a glass of the Liebfraumilch.

'Are there any German words in use in medicine, Sibylle?'

'The only one I know of is *Mittelschmerz*. It can occur half-way between your periods. When you ovulate and the egg pops out from the ovary, a spot of blood often comes with it and this can cause a little localised tummy tenderness. I have it quite often. It tells you on which side you've ovulated and – in me at least – it usually alternates. If it's on the right, it's a part of the differential diagnosis of appendicitis too.'

Afterwards we left the washing-up and the four of us did a Christmas crossword.

Next morning I caught the train back to Devon.

CHAPTER FOUR

From the train I watched a herd of cows roll by, oblivious to the catastrophe they were unleashing.

I bought tea and a sandwich from the trolley lady.

Would village-maid Mary have been more self-controlled? Had she, her lithe beauty draped in her ankle-length blue-and-red-patterned dress with its cord-tie, been espied by some foreign hero as she drew water at the well? And had his arts of persuasion or the glitter of his Roman gold tempted her?

'Loveliness exists only where the possessor is oblivious to her own loveliness.' So said Lessing … or someone. Yet were the young not entitled to err, to be impulsive, to barter their innocence and their purity?

Yet I *was* attractive and as I discovered myself more, I would become more authentic, more confident … even if also more artful. But was this vanity?

I am an only child and my parents were delighted to see me and to pamper me over Christmas.

To the question, 'And how is Newcastle?' I had no simple answer.

'Well, I like my subjects … '

Mummy of course, plumbed the topic of boyfriends.

'I'm seeing a young lecturer … but it's not overly serious.'

'Is he kind and well-disposed?'

'If not I would dispose of him … and not too kindly either.'

She smiled.

'Any thoughts on a career?' asked Daddy.

'Sibylle, a German medical student downstairs, is widely admired for her looks. Sophie asked her which specialty she might choose and she replied, "I am waiting to see which professor likes me."'

Daddy wrinkled his brow. 'It's not good to be too success-orientated ... a wolf with a lolling tongue.'

'Nor a sheep?'

'A lamb perhaps?'

'Not in today's world.'

At Midnight Mass, Daddy preached on 'wisdom'. He quoted Goethe; 'There is no noble crown – well-worn or ill-worn – which is not a crown of thorns.' And from the Bible, 'Haughty eyes and an arrogant pose I shall not endure, says the Lord.'

We ate our Christmas dinner off our nineteenth-century hand-decorated Bavarian plates, with holly, gold baubles and candles twinkling in the centre of the table.

Uncle Basil – Daddy's brother – called in for a brandy and some Christmas cake. He is a criminal lawyer – that is one who defends criminals, in case you were wondering – and he probed my choice of subjects.

'Mary's a dilettante,' Daddy defended me.

'Languages intrigue me ... even though they don't come easily.'

'Theology or physics, say, have well-trodden paths for debating or confirming hypotheses. Languages tie in nicely with history. Yet these newer psycho-eco-sciences ... it's like gluing moonbeams to soap bubbles.'

Later, Daddy said, 'Despite a firm friendship, when it

comes to personal matters, I feel I am more open with your uncle than he is with me?'

After a second bite of mince-pie, I said, 'I suspect there's a slight complex there ... inferiority is too strong, but something along those lines. His wife ran off with a gamekeeper, he was booted out from those chambers in Bristol, he nearly went bankrupt and he's now with that know-all Marlene woman.'

'Yet he could still trust me?'

'But like that game with a tower of wooden blocks where you remove them one at a time ... perhaps he fears that if he admits one thing – her showy airs say – then the whole stack will collapse?'

Daddy sipped his wine.

'You've lived in India, Saint Helena, France ... written two books?'

'But everyone's had disappointments, misfortunes. You just have to keep going from where you are.'

'Perhaps he feels a bit of a failure and his lack of openness is a defence? He does not want to admit it to you. He wants to keep a little pride. Does that make sense?'

Daddy took a slow breath. 'Mary, you're very perceptive.'

Back in Newcastle, it snowed. Brandling Park looked so beautiful with the trees all white when I walked from the flat over to the University.

I saw one guy there having a dispute with a cherry tree. It escalated and he started punching it. Diagnosis: too much Newcastle Brown Ale.

I signed up for a 'dig' in the Easter holidays. It was

to be in northern Israel and coincidentally not far from Tiberias where Herod Antipas had had his new palace built around 20 A.D. On the map I saw too the site of Magdala, marked by the Sea of Galilee.

Daddy was thrilled when I rang and told him and instantly sent me eight hundred pounds.

My subconscious mind worked its arcane magic. I dreamt that my breasts were being fondled by a richly-garbed Syrian secretary in the Tetrarch's palace. He gave me a thick gold ring with an exquisite apple-green chrysoprase in it, in exchange for a night together. The sex was impeccable. 'Who is this Tom?' he knitted his brows. 'You have no need to scrape the barrel, Mary.'

I woke up and then slept again. As a priestess to Baal, with an altar of stones on one of those 'high-places', I encouraged my wayward Israelite flock to tinker with or taste all manner of diverse carnal delights.

I joined the rowing club and so went out on the Tyne on Wednesday afternoons in a girls' 'four'. The river water looked like oxtail soup. Someone said that a cox had fallen in and died, because a lump of excrement had stuck sideways-on in his throat.

I still saw Tom most Saturdays, but it seemed to be static, going nowhere.

Otherwise the term consisted solely of work.

Sophie said that the maximum amount of study you could satisfactorily do in a day was about five hours. Quite a conversation-stopper this, since I had never seen her do more than two.

She did have one burst of activity; an attempt to write a spy novel.

'There are two Russian moles working in Paris, but neither knows the other is a mole. So they have an affair, each hoping to milk the other, but Popsy Beaufort – my honey-trap seducer – has simply trapped a wasp with no useful juice in it.'

A timid boy in the Modern Greek beginners' set had some form of mental breakdown, after which he dropped out. I had never spoken to him and felt a bit guilty that I had not asked him to join our group for coffee after lectures.

Clearly a loner, his name was Osric Fairless. There was some story about him stealing a cushion too. He stuck in my mind and I said a prayer for him.

A few days before the Easter break, as I walked through Brandling Park, I espied a spindly urchin slinging a briefcase under a bush. I recovered it. Inside were note-books, a folder of essays, some chocolate biscuits and a wallet. It belonged to Professor Jones.

I went to the Politics Department and knocked on his door. As I entered and he saw the briefcase, he stood up, grasped my hand and thanked me profoundly.

'It was snatched from the passenger seat of my car whilst I was filling up at the petrol station.' After combing through it, he said, 'I think all that's missing is the money from the wallet.'

'The cheque-book gave me your name. In fact,' I added with a touch of dry humour, 'I almost tore the last cheque out from the back and bought myself a car.'

He gave a half-laugh then bent forwards. 'Well I wish you had. It was a paying-in slip.'

I laughed.

'What's your name?'
'Mary Fleet. General Arts.'
'Thank you Mary. Thank you very much.'

CHAPTER FIVE

In Israel we worked in a knee-deep, neatly dug hole, thirty-yards by thirty, in which smaller squares had been sunk lower. The soil was dry and full of tiny stones. We used trowels and sieves, brushes and magnifying glasses and learnt the basics of good excavation practice and how to distinguish the different strata.

The Levant is awash with ancient artefacts; coins, pottery fragments, nails, the odd hair-pin and such like. A broken clay jar with a lump of blackened silver inside, we guessed to be a hoard of coins melted by a fire. Our finds were numerous, but all in a poor state.

I wore sandals, a short loose frock in pastel blues and greens with its cuffs rolled back and a wide-brimmed sun-hat.

We took a boat trip on Lake Galilee together with a group of German pilgrims. On the eastern shore, we lunched at a falafel bar beneath date-palms and terebinths and eyed the cliff where the herd of demon-possessed swine had supposedly plunged to their deaths. By the time we tied up again at Tiberias, we could almost recite the Lord's Prayer in German.

A second outing was to Jericho, famous for its walls and its balsam trees. We tasted the salt grass of this below-sea-level region and paddled in the milky-green waters of the River Jordan.

We were bivouacked on a kibbutz and as we ate kebabs round the camp-fire one evening, we discussed the *prutot*, the small bronze coins we had unearthed in great numbers, known usually at home as 'widow's mites'.

Glenis, our supervisor, said that one would typically have bought a pomegranate. If my Biblical heroine had wished to haggle over a dyed scarf or an amphora of wine in the market-place say, she would have needed the Roman silver coins, the denarii.

At the start of the summer term, Tom called to say we were ended.

Though unsurprised, I had not entirely seen it coming. I remained unflustered and civil and thanked him for the times we had shared.

'You didn't send me a card from Israel?'

'No. I know.'

I thought he looked a bit uneasy or shame-faced and wondered if some grubby girl had sunk her claws into him?

Anyway, pride and pique were kept on a leash, until he came back. 'Could I have that football book back, please?'

'No,' I shouted. 'Get out.'

Sophie had not batted an eyelid. 'They say that a boy and a girl's coming together resembles two flowers intertwining. You lacked any bright buds and he was just a leafless stalk.'

I sucked my cheeks in. 'You could have dropped a hint.'

'I did … but it's hard to be totally sure. Ultimately only those involved really know.'

'There was no thrill … no tingle.'

Still, it was exam season, which meant work, although one evening we went to *The Admiral Collingwood*.

'It's an old pub this.'

'Yes. Didn't Richard the Lionheart drink here?'

Sophie's class-mate Ed ambled in. He spent most of his time in bars, wrote some guff in the exams and yet seemed sure of a pass. He fancied a girl named Tessa, but expected her to do the running.

'You *should* make an effort,' said Sophie, 'and find some decent clothes. You think you're above vanity, but girls aren't.'

He took off his anorak and a bandage poked out from the undone cuff of his right shirt sleeve.

'What happened?'

'I was held by this police dog ... the size of a Himalayan bear.'

Ed and his pals had been spraying a graffito on a synagogue wall, when some volunteers with supplies for the next day's soup kitchen had spotted them and given chase.

'Delivering tomato soup *at midnight*? Then this police van drew up.'

I eyed an oil painting on the wall. 'Who was Admiral Collingwood?'

'Nelson's second-in-command at Trafalgar,' said Sophie.

'Nelson,' began Ed, 'had one wife and an affair with Emma Hamilton. So his whore-ratio was one to one.'

Céline Seddon joined us. 'Shall I order?'

We've ordered,' I said.

'Ed? Shall I be Hermes?'

'Or herpes?' It was my voice, but I had not thought it.

Céline stopped briefly in her tracks and glared at me.

Sophie smothered a giggle.

When Céline returned, she asked, 'Sophie, how *bona fide* it is that Prof Jones writes comments on your essays in Welsh?'

'You wrote "*Cui bono?*" on my last one.'

'Does Prof Jones not mark according to the essayist's leanings?' I ventured.

'This is not the Age of Chivalry.'

'Obviously.' I raised my eyebrows.

'Don't look down at me,' Céline breathed sweetly.

I kept my eyebrows level. 'We all have areas where we excel.'

'You're not some goddess.'

'Oh?'

Céline eyed her glass. It was of tough translucent plastic, designed not to be smashed and used as a weapon.

I gave a conciliatory smile. 'Shall we end this sparring?'

She waved the white flag.

'Then all's well with the world.'

Ed swung his glasses off and rubbed his drooping lids, before fingering his stubble in deep thought. 'To quote Tacitus, "You know not my son by how little wisdom the world is governed."'

That evening Sophie and I sat up.

'Ed's middle name is "Miami".'

'Was he conceived there?'

Sophie grinned.

'It could have been Bangkok?'

'That "Tacitus" tag actually comes from a Swede,

Earl Oxenstierna. His son, due to represent their country at the Peace of Westphalia, said that he felt too inexperienced to negotiate with the seasoned diplomats of Europe. Then his father said that line to him.'

'So not some matured wisdom, just spontaneous advice?'

We made some toast and another round of tea.

'"Toasted bread" Céline calls it. She went to a minor public school.'

My flat-mate spread butter and marmalade liberally onto her toast. Gone were the pumpkin seeds and the carrot juice. She had looked a touch greenish at one point and Sibylle had suggested 'chlorotic anaemia', a condition seen only in young women. Clearly marmalade on buttered toast was the cure.

Sophie inspected her nails, then poked her cheek with a pencil. 'My course? Is it just an ungilding of the philosophic pill or is it all flub?'

I sipped my tea. 'Would you go the whole hog?'

'Ninety per cent of the hog. Perhaps leave the snout.'

'It does sound a bit of a fixed repertoire. What about the nipples?'

'Intelligence implies some flexibility. Only a dullard sees everything as black or white.'

I nodded.

'I'm changing courses.'

My eyes widened. 'Oh?'

'To Japanese.'

I put my tea down.

'It's been in my noddle for a while.'

I pondered it. 'I think it'll do you good.'

'So good-bye to Céline and her conformist hog-wash.'

'Tell her when you're feeling *rasher*.'

'I would definitely like to ... the narcissist.'

'Or nasty cyst?'

'Prof Jones is speaking to his buddy in Oriental Studies and fixing it for me.'

I sat my last exam on June the first.

Four of our neophyte archaeologist set went for a paddle in the sea at Tynemouth. Like kids, we started splashing one another and were so dripping wet, that a café owner barred our entry.

We sat on a bench and Freddie – who used the f-word before almost every noun – went to fetch ice-creams. Sheelagh said, 'When he comes back, let's count the words he says before the f-word.'

He arrived and bent down to hand us our 99's, but the cord round his neck which held his flat key, caught on the back of the seat and nearly beheaded him.

We sniggered. The tally was zero.

Sheelagh read a text message. 'My mum says that in Málaga the water's *only* twenty-three degrees.' Here it had yet to reach twelve.

James's car ran out of petrol and three of us had to push it half a mile to a garage. Yet the sun shone and that day everything seemed like good fun.

In Jesmond, my mobile pinged. Professor Jones asked that I ring him. I was intrigued. He would have obtained my number through the Arts Faculty secretary.

'Mary? Heddwyn Jones here. Are you able to come to my house in Gosforth this evening?'

'Er, yes. For dinner?'

'No. I would like you to meet someone.'

'I'm curious.'

'Splendid.'

A sixth sense told me to make an effort.

My long dark hair I coiled up into a neat top-knot. I trimmed my eyebrows, applied two thin arcs of eyebrow pencil, a merest hint of blusher to my cheeks and a delicate dark-pink lipstick. I affixed neat silver ear-rings to my ear-lobes, then pulled on black tights, a white underskirt and a white cotton long-sleeved blouse with a turned-down lace collar and a small bright-red bow. On top of this went a flared short-sleeved low-neck-line grey linen dress with a wide soft black leather belt and lastly plain black leather shoes with pointed toes. This knee-length dress – which I had used for my university interviews – had a quite crisp crinkly feel to it. The intended effect was to be classy and just a teensy bit sensual.

'Mirror, mirror, on the wall, who is the fairest of us all?'

'Who's taking you out?' asked Sophie. 'The Sheikh of Timbuctoo?'

'Close.'

'Come on. Spill the beans.'

'Aha. You would need to sit down first, because if I told you, you would collapse.

Oh, I forgot the perfume.' I applied a few dabs behind my ears.

Sophie asked, 'Chanel No. 5?'

'Do I look like I can afford that? Canal Number 1, more like.'

My mother had also been attractive in her youth. One should capitalise on one's figure before it faded.

I felt both confident and happy.

Prof Jones lived just around the corner from the South Gosforth Metro station, in a row of stone Victorian terrace-houses which faced a spread of tidily pruned trees and bushes. The houses were quite spacious, with neat lawns in front, thick solid iron railings on a stone plinth and with two stone steps up to the front door.

'What delightful dwellings.'

'Built from 1864 to 1868; from left to right.'

My coat was taken and I was shown into the airy front room with its high ceiling, flower-filled old iron grate, replete alcove bookcases, grand piano and bay window.

The Professor introduced me to his nephew, Malcolm.

We nodded, smiled, shook hands and sat down on the old leather sofas. As I crossed my legs, my underskirt showed briefly, until I pulled my dress down over it.

On side tables were three antique porcelain statuettes and two elegant art deco lamps. On the walls were original paintings of Venice and of early railways.

'Mary, I am sure this is all a bit of a mystery to you, but Malcolm runs a small film studio. It deals mostly with commercial presentations, but also some media advertising.'

I gave a slightly quizzical smile.

'And with this, comes the occasional opening for a pretty girl.'

I inhaled. 'It's very kind of you to think of me Professor.'

'One good turn deserves another, Mary.

You are extremely winsome and … well, we must ask Malcolm … but I think he may be able to offer you something?'

I am sure I blushed.

Malcolm grinned. 'My uncle still has good taste, I see?'

I think I shook my head rapidly and minimally in bemusement.

'Mary, would you mind walking up and down a few times … just casually?'

I stood up and endeavoured to walk naturally and easily, imagining I was an actress going to meet her boyfriend in the park.

The upshot – stated over mocha coffees and a biscuit – was an offer based on a contract on their books for a forty-second coffee advert for television. It required one player, an attractive young woman. He apologised that the fee would be a rather paltry three hundred pounds, plus the return train fare to Carlisle. They would do my hair when I arrived, but the clothes I had on would be good … in fact, exactly what was needed.

I hid my delight. The novelty, the experience, the tantalising possibility of knock-ons? I nodded my assent.

'You must not in the meantime colour or cut your hair, tan or darken your skin in any way, nor have botulin derivatives injected into your lips … or indeed anywhere.

This Monday, ten o'clock?' He wrote down the address.

As the Metro train rattled back to Jesmond, I wondered

if this had all seemed too easy? Surely a formally trained actress would be *de rigueur* for such a *rôle*, even if it were 'just a coffee advert'? Or were they just being thrifty? Or did another sting lurk in the tail? Malcolm had struck me as a bit of a smoothie.

Yet Mary of Magdala would give it a shot, since excepting her physical attraction, nothing else she might do would earn her more than a few of those widow's copper coins.

Back in the flat, Sophie came out of her room wearing a medium blue kimono with an obi – a broad sash – of purple silk round her waist. Her hair, done up in a pile, had two knitting-needles stuck through it. She looked both quaint and delightful.

'Am I being stupid?' She bent forwards and laughed.

I laughed too and we embraced, holding one another for some seconds and ending with a brief kiss on the lips. We were not Lesbians, but a real bond had grown between us and suddenly ... we were both going somewhere.

'You look lovely,' I said. 'The kimono really suits you.'

She smiled happily.

CHAPTER SIX

In an ultra-modern architect-designed mansion near Carlisle, I met Malcolm Lacey and Cathy, his continuity girl.

We first practised my five short sentences, adding such nuances and inflections as might convey enthusiasm and conviction.

Then in the glistening, marble and steel space-age kitchen with its yellow cupboard doors, we rehearsed my three positions, one turn and one short walk. Facial expressions and hand movements needed to be a little exaggerated, Malcolm explained, so as not to seem inexpressive or bland. 'If you film ordinary behaviour it comes across as timid or inert. Your actions need to be ... not caricatured, but a bit intense, a touch larger than life or else they appear feeble.'

I was made up by Cathy and then we brought it all together and actually made the coffee.

The film crew arrived, four cheerful old sweats in jeans and T-shirts. They set up two Klieg lights, an elaborate video-camera, a furry microphone on a tripod, monitors, cables and a clapper-board. We shot the production of this earth-shatteringly good cup of coffee six times.

As if touched by some genie, I felt blithe and radiant and all seemed to run with barely a hiccough. With editing, Malcolm was sure it would be of the required standard. 'There's a nice light whimsical air about you,' he conceded.

Afterwards he took me to a coffee-shop.

'That went swimmingly, Mary. We've had worse professionals ... a lot worse. My uncle has been very good to my widowed mother – his sister – and he asked, if you were suitable, if I had anything?'

'Well, I enjoyed it.'

'On Wednesday we're making another television advert, this time for a washing powder additive and the girl contracted will cost three thousand pounds. Will you do it for another three hundred?'

'Of course.'

'Luckily we haven't signed her yet. You would need to wear something more homely. *Haute couture* and household chores don't mix well, even on television.'

I gave him my physical measurements and even though he seemed keen to touch my shoulder and bottom, I suffered it, since this all seemed too good an opportunity to miss.

And so on Wednesday, in the kitchen of an old biscuit warehouse, with my hair in a long school-girlish plait and a bright but simple red skirt and orange blouse, I busied myself throwing clothes into a washing machine and adding the magic liquid, all with a happy smile ... as one would of course if using this particular brand.

That evening, he gave me my cheque for six hundred and thirty pounds and drove me to Carlisle's Citadel Station.

There in the car, as rain rattled on the roof, he asked if he could give me a kiss? I gave a wary smile, but allowed him a brief peck on my right cheek.

'Mary, I want to see you.' There was urgency in his voice.

I touched his forearm and said with a forlorn smile, 'Perhaps another time? It's been nice working with you.'

He grimaced, knowing that this meant, 'No.'

I climbed out and went to catch my train.

Next day the exam results were published. I had passed in all subjects, though none with distinction. I bumped into my tutor who said, 'I wouldn't cut it that fine again.' My 'A' level grades – three 'C's – had been exactly what I needed. I seemed always to just scrape through.

I gave my silent thanks to God. I cuddled Titus, my old Teddy Bear and quoted the Prophet Malachi: 'For you who fear my name, the sun of righteousness shall rise ... with healing in its wings.'

Our Greek teacher, Niko Chloros, had fixed a summer job for me with his sister Katia and her husband, working at their restaurant near Kalamata in the Peloponnese. Thus three days later, I found myself rushing about, clearing tables or serving little tubs of the local olives with cheese and coarse bread or perhaps a kleftico. I fell asleep dead tired each evening from the heat, the different climate and the work, in a house in the village owned by Xenia, an old dame with a toothless smile.

A bank balance in the black meant you were not enjoying yourself enough; so said Socrates ... or someone. So I hired a car and with Cora Agathangelou – a seasonal worker from Thebes who sold sunshades and ice-creams on the beach – drove to Pylos, Sparta, Mycenae and Corinth, where we climbed on ancient tumbledown stones or sat amid mauve flowers under gnarled old trees to eat our picnics.

Everything seemed to be touch and go, but there were no calamities, though we had feet like raw meat-balls from walking and the insects found our insect-repellent irresistible.

An aura of timeless antiquity had been sown here by Athena and Hecate, the goddesses of wisdom and magic.

When I arrived home in early August, we had acquired a new cleaning girl. This busty and curvy young Russian, who came three times a week, had – to my mind at least – a quite evident underlying coarseness. I noticed that she subtly flaunted her physical attributes in front of my father and though he and Mummy were very close, middle-aged men can become oddly infatuated. He also eyed her furtively from behind a number of times.

Mummy had suggested that she and I take a last-minute cheap break in Tunisia to which Daddy gave his enthusiastic approval.

That afternoon I found myself alone with Elena. I was reading at the kitchen table and she, whilst doing the washing-up, was talking about this and that in a way intended to tell me what a sweet and nice person she was.

I closed my book. 'You just leave my father alone.'

She spun round abruptly. 'What the hell are you talking about?'

'I see your game. Have an affair with him, then poor Babushka's poorly so you need to go home ... but you can't live without him. So he goes too. Then he needs to buy a flat for you both which has to be in your name because of Russian law ... then you change the locks?'

Her face went rigid, contorted with fury.

I thought I might need to seize a chair and wield it like a lion tamer, but instead had just to endure a string of obscenities of which the gist was, 'You effing English bitch and snob.'

Finally she smashed some plates on the floor, grabbed her jacket and bag and we never saw her again.

Tunisia was a relaxing, lazy, pool-side holiday.

In mid-August, whilst hanging out clothes in the rectory garden, I received a call out of the blue from an outfit called Oberon Films. Ellie Binks, secretary to some director or other, asked if I would like to audition for a small non-speaking part in a spy film?

I tried to sound casual, but said yes, I would like that.

She sent me the details and in Mummy's twelve-year-old Fiat Panda, I drove to Sussex and to a house near the delightful little town of Cuckfield.

The property was a large Georgian mansion, possibly an old rectory though with much money spent on it. There were no company signboards and it had the air of being a private dwelling. I pressed the intercom, was greeted and the electrically operated gates swung open. I drove along the gravel drive, wound round a hedge and parked between what had been the bishop's stable and two expensive sports cars.

I had given thought to my dress. Long slits in dresses or skirts, apart from being vulgar give the impression that you are desperate. I had settled on a pleated blue-and-red tartan skirt which came to mid-knee level, a thinnish white cotton blouse with a narrow crimped collar and the usual black tights and shoes.

A slim fellow in his mid-forties approached and opened my car door for me.

I climbed out and smiled.

He introduced himself as Nick Yates, which was the director's name Ellie had given to me.

He had a short bristly beard and though 'haggard' was too strong a word, there was something a little uneasy or unhealthy about his persona.

'The coffee advert didn't lie. You are very pretty, Mary.'

I gave a second smile, which I hoped seemed friendly, though may have been a trifle awkward and we walked together to the impressively large front door and entered the house.

As he led the way through the spacious hallway with its two enormous oriental vases, he said, 'My wife and daughters have gone to Brittany for a fortnight, so it's do-it-yourself with the drinks.'

It seemed odd that I was seemingly the only person to be auditioned.

I followed him into the kitchen and he set the coffee percolator going.

I could not behave like some dumb adolescent, so I remarked on the lovely house and the rolling countryside thereabouts.

'It is a lovely spot ... the southern slope of the Weald ... open, arable farming mostly. Milk? Sugar? Cake?'

'Yes, no and yes, please.'

We moved through into the huge lounge, again high-ceilinged, modern and minimalist in its décor, where he waved me to a sofa.

He himself remained standing. 'This film we're planning, *The East German Renegade*, is based on a book by a Russian lass, Natalia Pastukhova and is set in the nineteen-fifties ... the earlier part of the Cold War.'

I nodded appreciatively, trying to absorb the overall scheme.

He picked up a stapled script from a side-table and sat down beside me, so close that we were brushing one another. I was careful not to flinch.

'The part I have in mind for you is set on a lonely railway station at dusk. You are seated on a bench wearing a fairly drab trench coat and lady's leather boots ... but still looking very pretty and subtly sexy ... '

I leant forwards to pick up my cake plate and fork whilst he continued.

'A man appears – in fact the lead actor – who strolls past you, returns, sits down a little way from you on the bench and after looking round, eyes you and you slide a small envelope across to him.'

'And that's it?'

'Yes. Approximately thirty-two seconds.'

He put an arm round my shoulders.

I knew it was to be a ten and half million dollar production and it included two quite big names.

This was a crossing the Rubicon moment.

The sofa was a low soft dark-green leather one, very suitable for accommodating bodies horizontally.

He pulled me towards him and tried to kiss me forcefully on the lips.

I held him gently at bay. 'Just a minute, what's the deal here?'

'You get the part ... if you'll spend the night with me?'

I felt temptation battling with revulsion. 'And what guarantee do I have of that?'

'We'll sign the contract and you can put it into your bag. The shooting of your scene – that's scene 14a – should be on September the sixteenth or seventeenth.' He pulled me towards him and forced a kiss onto my lips. 'Eight thousand pounds.'

Mary of Magdala had perhaps even been in the bed of Herod the Tetrarch himself – who knew – but it must have troubled her or she would not have had her seven devils. She would have been taught that God assays the soul. He weighs it and wishes to refine it. But the stubborn say, 'We do not wish to be refined. We are corrupt and like it so.'

I had had sex now five or six times with Tom. It was pleasant and I had started to discover how good it might be if done with the right balance of finesse and vigour. Tom and I had been quite gentle with one another and at least superficially affectionate, though lacking that deep bond which tells you, 'This is the one you're meant to be with.'

I drank some coffee. I wanted to resist, but it was the kudos and the prestige which drew me on, not the money.

I said coolly, 'All right ... then let's sign this contract.'

In an ecstasy of delight, he wrapped his arms around me and kissed me all over my face and then my breasts, hotly and wetly.

'Oh wonderful! I had a feeling you would.'

He disappeared to his office and returned with two three-page contract forms and a roller-ball pen. 'You're just down as "Ulla" in the cast list.'

He filled in the film title and all the other details and we both signed and dated both copies. I popped mine into my shoulder-bag.

'Ellie will send you all the details. It will be shot at a station on one of these preservation railways. We'll do all the make-up and stuff on site.'

He stood up. 'Right, business over ... time for pleasure?'

I pursed my lips and gave an oh-I-suppose-so type smile.

He ran up the stairs three at a time and I followed more sedately.

It was only three in the afternoon.

I took off my skirt and blouse and climbed between the sheets in my underwear. If the coffee advert had led to this, what might this lead to? But also at what cost? I suddenly swore inwardly, 'Oh damn it. Let's just get on with it.'

He was in beside me, naked. We turned to one another and he started to feel me here and there.

'I took so many screen-shots of that coffee advert. There isn't an hour goes by when I don't look at them. You are so unbelievably beautiful ... especially your face ... '

'We did a washing powder advert as well, but they haven't used that.'

'Not here, but it's been shown in Australia.'

'Oh?'

'And since then, that film studio's folded ... debts of over half a million.'

'Gosh.'

'The film industry's so tough ... sadly it often ends like that.'

'I became involved through the boss's uncle ... a very decent academic.'

'Is he a politics professor?'

'Yes. He made his name with early computer predictions, so the department just coasts now. No cutting-edge research to rake in sponsorship ... '

The talking ended and the sex began.

Yates turned out to be a bit of a shadow fighting itself. Despite the bravado, he had trouble getting going – which I did not mind at all – but he was embarrassed and I am pretty sure that he had to think dirty thoughts in order to spur himself on enough to deliver the goods.

I suppose I should have helped him, but I was not particularly keen to.

'For heaven's sake, grip it girl,' he urged.

As inexperienced as I was, I knew that I was not the cause of the problem ... merely the catalyst for renewal.

Covered in sweat, as if he had run a Marathon, he finally got over the hill.

We put our clothes on loosely and went to drink water, then had more coffee with bread and cheese, before a second round. Despite finding my physique stimulating, it was as if he was trying to prove something to himself.

Sat at the kitchen table – again – I recalled the prophet Micah. 'He has shown you what is good and what is needful for you, which is to act justly, to love kindness and to walk humbly with God.'

What other whore today, would sit there thinking of the Bible? Oh sod it. Why did God want to restrict us like this? Why were sexual acts so critical, so ... imbued with a life-and-death significance?

A he-man might have aroused me, but not this pathetic two-dimensional ghost. When he sensed that I was wearying of his efforts, he threw himself into a frenzy of exertion – because I suppose he felt humiliated – and when for the third and final time – and after endless failed attempts – he struggled over the brink, he asked me why I had not gasped? Had I not sensed a climax? Had it not been good?

I left at six o'clock and arrived home just before ten.

My mother asked, 'Well?'

I gave her a nice smile. 'They've given me a part ... only a small one though.'

'Oh wonderful dear.' She gave me a tight cuddle. 'My baby ... a film star.' She almost wept with joy.

CHAPTER SEVEN

When sixteen, I had been the narrator for our school Christmas play. *All that Glitters is not Gold* had been a parody on *The Merchant of Venice*.

In a yellow dress with a grey belt, white socks with patterned garters and a straw hat, I – Lucia – had stood behind the footlights as the curtain rose had recited the prologue.

'Our tale this night, in Venice set
Is grim but bright, but first to whet
Your senses, comes a serenata –
No dusty fugue nor dry cantata –
Nay, gut and rosin sweet shall play,
Whilst tambourine, beribboned, gay,
Shall lend her rings to barcarolle.
See, lo our players, here they stroll.'

After a simple canzonetta, the daughter of the merchant entered and – with a hand on her breast – told the audience in confidence, 'I'll sigh not for a shepherd; no not I. Here comes the Doge's son, a dim but haughty knave.' As she winked, the minstrels and I withdrew to the wings, leaving Hayley to lure Stephen into a wistful if contrived tryst.

In the second act, Sarah Emerson and I performed a *pas-de-deux* in a tavern scene. We actually took two lessons with a dancing teacher to learn it exactly and were rewarded with one exuberant critic saying we were 'extraordinarily Terpsichorean'.

If a bit clumsy and unpolished in places, the three performances had dashes of gaiety and humour.

I remember uttering the concluding two couplets.

'We trust you have liked our "Italianata",
Its follies, its riches, its inamorata;
Who now shall all be put to bed,
"The night is young," as Eros said.'

CHAPTER EIGHT

At evensong on the last Sunday in August, Daddy preached on the prophet Hosea. God told him to take a harlot to wife and to have children by her. She was called Gomer and after she had been faithless, he was told to go after her and bring her back; for this is what God does with His fickle and wandering sheep, wanting them to return and to obey.

Our church was Norman, squat, plain and cosy with its round crenellated arches and cream stonework; much more homely than the cold soaring Gothic chasms which came after.

Two half-year lambs grazed under the old yew in the churchyard, having found a break in the boundary fence. I tried to catch them, but in vain.

An aged spare fellow wandered in via the lych-gate.

Spotting me he explained that he had come in search of his sister's grave.

'She was only one. I so wish she had lived.' We sat on the stone bench. 'Selfish really ... for then I would have had a deeper understanding of girls.'

I asked, 'Are we so mysterious?'

He smiled. 'Not now ... but it's too late.'

'Oh.'

I sensed a man whose enthusiasm for life had slowly drained away as he discovered that its rewards were few.

'I once courted a well-to-do girl, but she ran off to Canada. Then I made a poor girl expectant. Had that happened to the rich girl, I would have wedded her and so – as it seemed wrong to distinguish on grounds of wealth – I married the poor girl.'

'That was very principled.'

'We were not in love and it was a mistake.'

'Though a very charitable one?'

'We had three children and are still together ... but we seldom speak.'

'That's so sad ... but I suppose it's quite a common story?'

'Nature is clever. Women see the wider picture ... a home, income, a kind husband? Boys are infatuated in their youth with the physical side of it and by the time we understand, it's too late.'

'That's a bit depressive?'

'True.' He gave me a kindly smile. 'And it is not always like that. I knew a lovely girl once who was mad about some moron and when he ignored her, she was in despair. She didn't know what to do.'

'So what did she do?'

'She begged in vain ... and then just had to accept it.'

We walked through the unmown grass.

'A girl in this village is desperate for children. When her boyfriend grew cool, she said, "Would it not be lovely if we had babies?" That betrayed her hidden motive ... so then he scarpered in double-quick time.'

His sister's headstone, quite small and tilted over, lay covered in green moss, fallen pine needles and catkins.

I left him alone.

Next day, I accompanied Daddy to tea with the new vicar in the next parish, Gemma LeCocq and her partner Berenice.

'LeCocq?'

'It's a Channel Islands' name,' explained Daddy.

'It's almost French. *J'aime le coq*,' I said. 'Is she the tom?' I was almost in hysterics.

'Look, just get over it before we arrive.'

Two scary African masks, carved from ebony, glared at me as I sat on the sofa. Daddy inspected the stuffed toucans with their large colourful beaks.

'We bought them in Guyana on our honeymoon,' said Berenice. 'They are so sweet and friendly, but can barely fly. We thought of writing a book about them.'

'But that too might not fly,' I thought.

Daddy spoke softly of the Creation's extent and wonder. 'Each star they now believe, has a very unique structure ... and there are trillions of them.'

Our tubby hostess had a number-one haircut and wore a pink woolly over her black blouse and dog-collar, a short black skirt and open-mesh tights. She wished the church's focus might be more on the relief of human suffering than on the Creation.

There was a pause which someone needed to fill.

'Suffering though, can bring us closer to God,' I said.

This contention seemed to baffle our hosts.

'Virtue only has meaning if there's a struggle with temptation,' I reasoned.

Everyone seemed dumb-struck.

'Hardship, drudgery ... they give us depth.'

Daddy said, 'The name "Berenice" – as mentioned in Acts – is probably a Macedonian corruption of "Pheronice", "Bearer of Victory".'

Berenice poured the tea whilst Gemma fetched the

pizza slices from the oven.

For the grace, Daddy recited the 'Hail Mary'.

We tackled the pizza pollo triangles, which were excellent.

'How can Mary be the mother of God?' asked Berenice.

'Well,' Daddy explained, 'the early Greek fathers argued that in John's gospel, Christ is said to be the Word and the Word was in the beginning and the Word was God. Therefore since Mary bore Christ, she is also the mother of God.'

'Hmm. Very Byzantine.'

We skated past Psalm forty-five where the 'King' is almost certainly Ahab and the 'Daughter of Tyre' Jezebel. We pirouetted on a Greek noun where doubt existed as to whether it should have a single or a double lambda. Then with a double-flip we ended up with one of Gemma's hobby-horses, 'wealth redistribution'.

I am not egalitarian and so in spite of Daddy's treading on my foot, I felt compelled to say, 'Life for everyone will consist of instants of happiness set amid struggles and trials. Devotion is about dissociating yourself from earthly or wrong pre-occupations ... not about anaemic artefacts ... such as bank balances.'

I knew that Daddy was cross as he struggled to rephrase this, like a lawyer saying, 'I'm sure what my client really means here is ... '

After a bit of flannel, we set off home.

'Well, what a diplomatic *tour de force* that was?'

I saw Gemma as a shallow yet abrasive trend-led stereotype. I almost called her a '*dick*-tator', but this was evidently not the moment for humour. 'I'm not sorry. She's a hoaxer.'

There was no reply.

'She made the standard mistake of those with paranoia ... seeing everything as personal.'

'Well, you gave her every excuse.'

Another few minutes passed.

'Think of Rachael, stealing the idols from her father's house? The purpose isn't clear, but ... '

'There's a lot that isn't clear in Genesis.'

'But is it because Laban needs to be taken down, to be shrunk?'

'Well you certainly gave LeCocq some conflict. What was it, "Using the flag of compassion to justify criminals ... "?'

'Then Laban pursues Jacob's lot to retrieve these things and in her tent she won't move off the sack because she says she's having a period? As if he would be fobbed off with that having just galloped over a few thousand miles of desert, but he knows ... '

I was not going to win here, so I gave up and we walked on in stony silence.

Monks meditate. They do not quibble over the edicts or rules which God has laid down. Nor – even if her mind were a touch distorted – had my fair heroine and temptress, Mary of Magdala.

I took Daddy's elbow, spun him round and put my arms round him. 'I'm sorry.'

We looked at each other without deceit. His brow gradually cleared. Then a thought, tenuous at first, gelled in his mind. 'Mary, did you get rid of Elena?'

'Yes.'

He took a slow deep breath, then hugged me. With our heads side by side, he whispered softly, 'Thank you.'

Mummy bought a new car, so I took over her old Panda and drove up to Newcastle three weeks before the start of term, where – mostly wearing a well-worn black denim skirt and an over-sized red woolly – I applied my nose to the grindstone of the coming academic year's studies; Renaissance Italy, Modern Greek Level 2 and Phoenician.

'Phoenician?' asked Sophie. 'What's that?'

'It's an early Aramaic or Canaanite language.'

'What happened to the Arabic?'

'Arabic Level 1 is only offered on alternate years.'

'Oh. But what can you do with this ... what is it? Phoenician?'

'Well it's related to Biblical Hebrew and to an extent to modern Arabic.'

'Oh.'

'*Yom* for example, means "day" in all of them.'

My antics with Nick Yates did not trouble me unduly, though a subtle lessening of my impassive or happy-go-lucky nature had perhaps come about. But was this just a part of growing up?

There was also, still no sign of anyone I might really fall in love with. No one set off a quiver down my spine.

Anyway, without losing heart, I pushed on with my studies and most days went for a swim.

One morning I had to meet my tutor, but the rain was torrential. Sophie had a tough canvas-backed blue plastic mack with a hood, so I nipped into her room to borrow it.

It was a bit loose on me, but also lop-sidedly heavy. In the deep right-hand pocket I found a huge bunch of keys, forty at least. I hung it back on its peg.

The East German Renegade – screened in mid-October – though more than breaking even for its sponsors, was not a huge success. My part, unspoken and fleeting, no one seemed to notice. I did not mind. The entertainment world is very much a roulette wheel.

In early November the door-bell rang and a woman whom I took to be in her mid-thirties – though was actually twenty-six – introduced herself as Jade.

'I'm a representative for "Equate", the actors' trades union.' A fake smile flickered across a face devoid of charm.

I invited her in, in case she had anything useful to tell, though refrained from offering her tea.

We sat down and she took a folder out of her bag.

'Mary, you played a small part in this recent film *The East German Renegade*?'

'Yes.'

'Professional actors are supposed to be members of the union.'

'I was only an "extra" ... a non-speaking part.'

'You were more than an "extra". You were in a scene alone with the principal lead.'

Despite a second brief smile, I sensed a latent aggression in her tone.

'Well no one mentioned any need to be in a union.'

She smiled falsely yet again. 'Well ... water under the bridge, but in future you do have to register.'

I shrugged.

'My main purpose however, is to ask about your audition?'

'Oh?'

'It took place at Nick Yates' house in Sussex, I believe?'

'Yes.'

'Why there? Why not in the studio? Why were only you invited?'

'I've no idea. Convenience perhaps? Ask him yourself.'

'Why do you think he chose you in particular?'

'He just said that I was extremely attractive ... so appearance I guess.'

I was delighted to she how much she loved this.

Her jowly cheeks flanked a largish nose. Her eyes were small and her hands unusually large and she had a habit of resting her top teeth on her lower lip. Her hair was a pink-tinted bob.

She swallowed. 'May I be blunt? Did he make any sexual advances?'

I thought for a few seconds. 'No. And anyway, who are you to ask such personal questions?'

'So what *did* happen?'

'Well, he talked a bit about the film ... and the scene he had me in mind for. Then he asked me to walk up and down, sit in a couple of different poses?'

'With your legs splayed?'

I leapt up. 'Get out!'

She leapt up too. 'I bet he had sex with you, didn't he?'

I could see a fight coming, so I shouted for Sophie,

who – as her door was slightly ajar – I had no doubt had been listening. She appeared promptly and looked ready for action.

'If he does *Macbeth* and needs some witches, you'll be ... '

She flew at me, but Sophie stuck a leg out and tripped her up so that as I stepped back she stumbled onto her hands and knees.

As she stood up, Sophie asked if she liked lettuce, then mentioned a good plastic surgeon in the city.

This time she lunged at Sophie, but after a minute of mutual hair-tugging and kicking, we managed to push her down the stairs where she slipped and broke her arm and we had to call an ambulance.

I raided her handbag and discovered her full name and address; Jessica Crosby, 4 Slade Mews, Chelsea.

After she had been spirited off to hospital, Sophie said, 'Now that the film's been made and released, what has she to gain?'

'Perhaps he's bypassed her before ... or there's some other grudge behind it.'

'Yes. Forget the hokum about "a level playing-field". It'll be something personal.'

Later a policewoman appeared. An allegation of assault had been filed. Sophie and I made a joint statement saying that Jade had called out of the blue, raged about my selection for a film, become violent and had herself stumbled and fallen down the stairs.

The police lass was stolid and non-partisan, though very over-weight and inelegant. Gone were the days of prim stand-to-attention female officers.

'I think she's the one who gave James a parking ticket last year,' I said to Sophie.

'Could be worse. She could have sat on him.'

CHAPTER NINE

One chilly Sunday morning, I drove to North Shields for some sea air and solace.

I parked beside the Fish Quay and walked towards Clifford's Fort.

A local ragamuffin winked and I replied with a friendly grin.

Clifford's Fort is a coastal battery dating from the Anglo-Dutch wars, whose cannon had once enfiladed the Tyne estuary.

I hotched onto one of the wedge-shaped stone parapets which separate the embrasures and looked out beyond the little promenade at the fog hovering above a rough grey sea. The waves rolled in under this low-hanging mist to surge against the Black Midden Rocks or the breakwater and toss foam up into the air.

After a while, I sensed a second presence and so twisted round to peer over my shoulder.

'Mary?' inquired the dim figure, who stood five yards back.

I recognised him, though could not immediately place him.

'Osric. I was in your Greek set last year.'

'Oh yes.' I spun round, jumped down, took a few paces forwards and smiled. 'You left us? What are you doing now?'

'I work for a small engineering company.'

'Good. Do you like it?'

'Yes ... I enjoy doing things with my hands.' He gave

me a smile, tinged with sorrow.

'You joined us a little late didn't you?'

'Yes. I dropped the pure maths option after a week and swapped to the Greek.'

'I'm sorry we didn't ask you to join us for coffee sometimes … after lectures.'

He gave a sideways tilt of the head.

'So easy to be thoughtless?'

He nodded. 'Could we have coffee now?'

I felt outfoxed, the victim of some simple conjuring trick. 'Er … yes, I suppose so.'

As we drove in my car, up into Tynemouth, I spoke briefly of my summer job near Kalamata and the day out with Cora in 'Sandy Pylos'.

He recalled the two students he had shared a flat with in Elswick, each writing a crime story where the other figured as the baddy. 'The rooms were grim, Dickensian … they set the scene.'

We reached the clock-tower at the end of Front Street, parked and got out.

I was wearing an old woollen winter coat with chequered squares of purple and blue and a tie belt.

'Why did you swap over to Greek?'

'To be near you.'

I thought I might have misheard this rather husky reply, so I said, 'Which café? The Italian or the local?'

'I don't mind. This morning, as I climbed out of the bath, I had a eureka moment.'

'Oh? Did you slip on the soap?'

'I had a premonition that I would see you today.'

Osric was tall, quite thin, with a flattish face, large

ears and short hair. 'Can I kiss you?'

I sensed a strange flutter in my chest. 'Um ... a quick one if you wish.'

He kissed my brow. 'You are so statuesque, so pure. If I were Petrarch, you would be my Laura.' He was trembling.

This seemed a bit intense. Trying to lighten things, I teased, 'How's your sonnet writing coming along?'

His mildly fraught features or aura, confounded me. A part of me wanted to be tender, yet I also knew not to buckle. 'I think we should forget the coffee. I have a lot of work to do.'

A jogger stumbled past, gasping.

He seized my hand. 'I should have been brave, like a knight ... I see that now, but I thought you would not even look at me.'

I snatched my hand free. 'Look, I have *not* led you on.' I spoke quite sharply, though not as sharply as I had intended.

He looked downcast. 'No, I know,' he replied humbly. 'I'm sorry.'

I walked briskly away, leaving him motionless and moist-eyed.

Having acquired a battered old car, I now used most of my film-début money for the deposit on a shabby old house. An unloved terrace-house in Glenthorn Road, near West Jesmond's Metro station had been recommended by Sheelagh's aunt, a local estate agent. The roof was in good repair and the sash-windows had been renewed, but it needed redecorating and various bits and bobs fixing. Daddy stood as my mortgage guarantor and I thought to move in in the New Year.

One of the endless 'searches' assured me that the new high-speed rail line from London to Birmingham would not run through its back-yard; they had chosen the shorter route. Money for old rope.

An irregular apprehension about Osric beset me, but I put it down to some fluctuating hormonal upset. Yet at other times, I wondered? Was his invisible affection or need of me winging its way through the – what was it – the ionosphere? Being idolised might please your ego, but it can also breach an emotional bar.

Osric yearned for my love, whereas that up-himself sod 'Relief in Africa' – or 'relief in bed' more likely – had only sought after my vulva.

Sophie, who was now bent over her Japanese for an amazing six hours a day, sensed that I was restless. 'I can hear you rolling pencils along the desk instead of working.'

'I'm finding it hard to concentrate … especially in the evenings.' My stomach gurgled inopportunely.

'You're moping. Is it telling you something?'

'Like what?'

'A boy? Or the allure of the film world again?'

When I failed to reply, she probed, 'A boy?'

I looked at her, then sighed. 'Perhaps, but there's too much wrong with him.'

'Do you think he's not good enough?'

'No I don't think that,' I snapped, then added weakly, 'or do I?'

'"The moping owl does to the moon complain."'

'And what does the moon answer?'

74

'She doesn't. The wise moon stays silent.'

I nearly rang Nick Yates, but stopped short because my concocted excuse was too contrived for words.

As my finger hesitated over the call-button a second time, miraculously he rang me. Telepathy?

'Mary? I'm in Amble. Can you pop up this evening?'

His boat, moored in the Amble Marina, was a medium-size cabin cruiser, grey and white, sleek, plenty of chrome attachments and named ACTICA.

He met me on floating jetty 'E'.

'An odd name? Is it to do with acting?'

'No. It's an acronym; "Another Crazy Thing I Can't Afford". I bring her here each winter. Tomorrow they'll take her out of the water, scrape her and then put a tarpaulin over her.'

In the cabin he poured some juice and set about heating two microwave meals.

'Someone called Jade or Jessica Crosby came to see me.'

'And what did *she* want?'

'Well it started with her talking about the "Equate Union", but that was just a foot-in-the-door ploy. She wanted to know why you had given me the part of Ulla in the *Renegade*, especially as I had no drama school training? I replied that I believed it was because of my appearance ... '

He gave a brief hyaena-like howl. 'I bet she loved that?'

'She started to get quite nasty and asked whether anything *risqué* had occurred, so I tried to turf her out and she attacked me ... but with the aid of my flat-mate we got the better of her ... and then she fell down the stairs and broke her arm.'

Nick threw his head back and gave a muted cackle. 'She detests men for their lack of interest in her, but that repels them even more.

When her husband divorced her in Florida, the court ruled that he had to buy her a house to live in, so he bought her one in the middle of an alligator swamp.'

I too could not resist a laugh.

'So Miss Fleet, tagine … stewed lamb with apricots and spices, then strong coffee with unripe figs.'

I must have looked dubious. 'And the rum truffles?'

He sat beside me on the bunk-sofa and fingered the nape of my neck. 'Moroccan fare … there's a reason. A new film. I'll explain in a bit.'

I said how pleased I had been with my little scene in *The East German Renegade*.

Nick kissed me on the cheek.

'So Jade bears you a grudge?'

'She's auditioned unsuccessfully a number of times, but she just wasn't right for the parts … '

'And her looks aren't the greatest?'

'Her grandfather – an old repertory actor – pulled levers which gained her the odd supporting *rôle*, but … basically, she just can't act.'

I turned to face him. 'I could have dropped you in it.'

'I understand that.' He took my hand, but I gently withdrew it.

'Could you offer me something in … your new piece?'

'I think so. Two or three others will be at the audition, but so long as you don't make a hash of it … ? How's your French?'

'Quite good.'

'Luise – the girl in question – has to speak a few lines of French, although she's German.'

He drew the curtains and his arms encircled my shoulders. 'These bunks are very narrow, so only the most slender of my girlfriends has the pleasure ... '

I thought I was prepared for his exploits, but suddenly I knew I could not do it. I took hold of a forearm. 'Nick, I can't.'

'Can't? Why not?'

I put my face into my hands and breathed deeply. 'I'm not sure ... but I might be in love.'

'Oh dear,' he sighed. 'Some greasy Casanova or a brainless muscular Hercules?'

I only just held back my tears. 'Quite the contrary,' I said with a slight shudder, but thought, 'Someone shy and possibly self-abusing.'

'But you want the part?'

'I'll not accuse you of sexual misbehaviour.'

'So, blackmail?'

'No. I won't denounce you either way, after all I consented ... but Luise?'

'A nice kiss then ... and touch your hair and breasts?'

'All right.' I gave a wry 'I-suppose-so' smile.

Driving home, I stopped at the entrance to a farm track. In daylight, the fields, woods and little stone villages in rural Northumberland could be so peaceful, still touched by that air of solitude as in a less hectic epoch.

I trusted that Osric would be able to interpret my cold shoulder not as an absolute 'no', but as a demand that he change. I ought not to make it too easy for him.

I went behind a hedge for a wee and somehow amid the darkness and the brambles managed to lose a shoe. I just could not find it. This was insane. 'Damn,' I said as I trod on a thistle.

Breathing heavily, I leant on a stile. Should I be hard, like iron … or yield?

CHAPTER TEN

Asumi – a Japanese girl – and Sophie had cooked a curry. The Japanese use pudding rice, which I prefer to the harder long-grain type.

Japanese sounds are straightforward to an English speaker. Its simpler syllabic script had originally been devised for girls, Sophie stated, since less time was spent on their education.

'It also uses pictographs. The oft-quoted one is of three women under a roof, which signifies "an argument". The medieval scribes were men, so a secret little joke.'

Asumi explained that in Japan too, there is an acceptance of parallel lives as an antidote to the inflexibilities and formalities in the office or within your social circle.

'If I go shopping in Kobe in a Jane Austen muslin empire-line dress or in a Greek tunic – as Iphigenia or a Spartan maiden – no one will poke fun, since such fantasies provide a necessary release.'

This struck me as very peculiar, until I came across Eleanor Way.

Next day a message from Ellie gave the venue and the date for the audition.

I felt unusually anxious and I told Sophie about my encounter in Tynemouth.

'So, it *is* a boy?'

'Yes.'

'Why did he not ask you out earlier, if he's so screwed up?'

'Because he's nervous and thought I'ld refuse ... which I probably would have.'

'But at least he would have tried?'

I thought for a bit. 'We're all tested in different ways. Some have doubts or demons we can't even guess at.'

'Is he just teasing you ... or bluffing? Boys don't worship us like this today ... even the troubadours only pretended to.'

'It was not a leg-pull ... and I'm not exaggerating.'

'Or hallucinating?'

'No.'

She shrugged and we let it drop.

Most religions promote the benign thought, the good deed, but the Bible's stress is on obeying God. It is not about being philanthropic, but God saying; 'Do what I tell you and I will be with you and will shield you.' Serenity and contentment depend on your trusting Him, because you do not know the future, the road or the end-point.

Kierkegaard says: 'Life can only be understood backwards, but it has to be lived forwards.'

Gemma LeCocq and her kind see which side their earthly bread is buttered on and so – like the false prophets who opposed Jeremiah – propound soppy self-deceptions; placatory clichés. This is the way to an empty, pointless, self-scuppering existence. Saying the same as everyone else is the easy path; then you are not reviled.

I had half-read a biography of Sarah Siddons, the eighteenth-century actress. Enduring success depends on following the path laid down for you and only your instincts – or the Holy Spirit – will guide you.

I slept, then awoke from a strange dream where I fought over a great bone with someone who was very strong. It had mysterious letters carved on it. It was my fate to love him. Perhaps I did not want to, but I chose submission rather than face disaster. Gradually and imperceptibly my fears lessened and my chaos settled.

The Moroccan Plot is an adventure story based largely on fact. At the end of the nineteenth century, Kaiser Wilhelm the Second wished to undermine French interests in Morocco.

A German aristocrat from Oldenburg is taken from his ancient and noble regiment and given a junior staff officer post. A half of his land has been confiscated during Prussia's heavy-handed takeover of the weaker Germanic states. Embittered, he relays via his brave second cousin Luise, a secret plot to the French. It tells of the smuggling of weapons into Morocco – via the Sus Valley in the south – to arm two barbaric and unruly tribes in the High Atlas, who will then strike at French forts and garrisons.

I drove to the West Midlands, where I ate and slept in a top-notch hotel. In the morning I bathed and spent a lot of time titivating myself before putting on a casual though unusual dress – grey with a bold orange zig-zag above the hem – to give the impression that I had made only a minimum of effort.

As I checked out the receptionist asked, 'Did you enjoy your stay … and your dinner last night?'

'Umm … I don't remember.'

'Oh. Then at least it wasn't atrocious?'

At ten o'clock I crept into a dowdy provincial theatre

and sat in the gloom on the tenth row of the auditorium. Other aspirants were dotted around, whilst on the front row sat Emma Appleyard the producer, Jeanette the costume designer, Antony the locations advisor and Ellie, all with clip-boards on their knees and clutching pencils.

Nick stood on stage in a pool of light and read the lines of the French consul, as he auditioned a beefy Kafir for the part of Bou Hazar.

'Look ... it's too turgid. You're being insulted. You're seething ... let's feel it?'

Next were the punters for the *rôle* of General Gerhard von Dietz. 'Good. That smile was more menace than charm ... I liked it ... but clip your lines. You're a rigid uncouth salvo-firing Prussian.'

Then came Luise.

Eleanor Way, although an actress of some repute, seemed only to convey hauteur. She was rather wooden and being in her mid-thirties, a touch old for the part. Nick said, 'Eleanor, less of the R.S.C. accent ... and it's too forceful. A well-bred girl of 1895 ought to be more ... gentle.'

Her curvy body and 'well-developed' breasts could though be a box-office draw. Her reddish hair was tethered loosely, her teeth were neat, white and even and her skin looked smooth. I wondered which skin-care lotions she used? Not just soap I guessed? All I knew was that sunshine and smoking were bad for it.

Chloë Stoneley at twenty-three, had an amusing knack of getting the wrong end of the stick. She was though a bit whimsical and naturally intuitive in her reactions to others, but as to playing Luise, was she too nonchalant, too blasé? She was cute – though not beautiful – slender, blonde and with eyes widely spaced.

I was last up. I felt calm, yet far from confident. I remembered not to hurry my lines and to infuse a few twists into them.

When little, I had attended a private prep school – boaters with ribbons, elocution lessons and country dancing – a vestige of that distant world which this notional Luise might have inhabited. We said, 'All right,' not 'Okay', kept our backs straight and did not start eating things off our dinner plates until we had sat down.

Nick eyed me sharply. Despite our equivocal first liaison, I sensed that we trusted one another.

I sat down beside Chloë.

'You were good,' she said.

'We both have long necks ... perhaps they help us to look more elegant?'

'Most girls in Sunderland's night-clubs have pony-tails to show off their bare necks ... but their "poise" – if that's the word – undoes the advantage.'

'Do you live in Sunderland?'

'I was a student there.'

'I'm in Newcastle.'

'I can't say why, but I don't think Nick will choose Eleanor.'

Boxed food and bottles of off-the-shelf coffee arrived and the house lights went on.

'These all-day breakfasts are huge,' I said. 'It'll take me all day to eat it.'

Chloë and I shared one.

Eleanor drifted up with a hint condescension. She looked like a shop-window mannequin.

Nick came across. 'Girls, thank you for coming.'

'So, the blonde, the red-head or the brunette?' asked Eleanor.

'We're having a meeting tomorrow morning Eleanor, after which Ellie will write to you all.' He left.

'So, is he sitting on the fence?' She threw us a puffy half-smile. 'Or do we know something?'

Chloë went to the ladies and Eleanor whispered, 'Isn't she common?'

I read this as, 'I envy her more youthful and lithe physique.' I said nothing, though noted her silvery-green nail varnish.

She stalked off.

Chloë returned and as the afternoon's cohort of Thespian potentials trickled in, we went off to a coffee-shop.

Her only big part so far had been in *The Zeus Spy Ring* and she needed something to keep her career afloat.

'Nick promised that if not Luise, he would give me the lesser *rôle* of Dido.'

'So you're sure of something?'

'Oh … I shouldn't really have said that.'

'Don't worry. I won't tell.'

She bit into her croissant. 'Did you have to go to bed with Nick in exchange for a *rôle* in this thing?'

'No.'

'I did. I didn't mind, but it's just so awkward … he has some sort of impotency problem.'

'Oh?'

'Zoë Sims, who played the lead in *Ultra-Girl*, said the same.'

'It's odd that he wants to advertise it?'

'I wonder if he keeps a record of all the actresses he's shagged ... a sort of collection of trophies?'

'Has he a stick with notches carved in it?'

'Did you see that article by Jade Crosby in *Talking Pictures*?'

'No.'

'A Canadian actress – Kim Wiseman – said how much she enjoyed "working under" Nick, "loved the roll", "worked flat out" and so on. Full of near-to-the-bone innuendoes.'

'It sounds borderline libel. I've met this Jade. Plug ugly ... I suppose all she can do is snipe?'

'Eleanor was in *Ultra-Girl*. She said how much she loved playing Ceres ... almost that she *was* her.'

'*Was* her?'

'Well, identified with her, I suppose. She's so self-absorbed.'

'Chloë, "optimism" is our watchword. If a dog can have its day, so can we.'

In a nearby side-street Chloë folded herself into her snazzy little sports car, the type often referred to as 'the hairdresser's car'.

'Bye.'

Back in Newcastle, Sophie asked, 'How did it go?'

'Hard to tell. Lots of unknowns. Wheels within wheels.'

Sophie had swapped to Japanese because of the

uniqueness of its culture, its isolation and its seemingly picturesque eccentricity, though of course, all is not as pristine as it first appears.

'With all Sino-Tibetan races, camaraderie, serving or cheating your bosses, even honouring your spouse ... all rank far below family ties.'

I absorbed this. 'My duty to my parents would override any obligation to you Sophie, but I would not deceive you.'

'And that's the difference.

My great-uncle Jonah – a long-serving engineer with the Malay harbour authorities – had eventually wearied of all these secret loyalties and the languor of the East and returned in his old age to the Vale of Llangollen.'

The house in Glenthorn Road had been rapidly if basically repaired, decorated and rented out. With two bedrooms and a dormer-windowed attic, three cheerful geology students and one girlfriend moved in. Vivian, who wore tinted glasses, had a pigtail and gold ear-rings – like a Chinese pirate – and his girl Evelyn – who always seemed to go round in a cloak – took the main bedroom. The plumber had said to her, 'Any friend of Batman's is a friend of mine.' Dennis and Justin were rugged Rugby players. One took the back bedroom and the other the attic.

This made sense as it brought in enough to pay the mortgage and besides, I liked the flat in Otterburn Terrace and Sophie's company.

I called on the new tenants one wintry Saturday morning in early December, to ask if everything was satisfactory.

'Well,' said Dennis, 'Water's running through the tap and not through the roof, Justin's delighted with his "Attic" architecture ... '

'Then at least it's not Spartan,' I countered.

'His "lofty" ceiling is a full five feet above the floor and ... '

The postman appeared with a letter for me from Ellie Binks. I had told her that I intended to move here, but then forgotten to cancel it.

The part of Luise was mine.

'Good news?' asked Justin.

I nodded. The fee was seventy-five thousand pounds!

From Otterburn Terrace I sent an acceptance message to Ellie, printed off and filled in the contract form ready to post and then opened a book on medieval Naples.

My thoughts swung between the scholars, scribes and lutenists of the Neapolitan court and Osric. Why had he not come? Had he not sensed my inner surrender, my belief that now we should be together?

At seven in the evening, Justin rang.

Back-tracking, this is what had occurred.

Vivian and Evelyn were away. Justin and Dennis had returned from a Rugby match and a few pints at around six and discovered a broken kitchen window.

The intruder they guessed, had climbed over the back wall from the alley-way behind the house, dropped down into the little concreted yard, broken a glass pane, reached in to undo the catch, then raised the lower half of the sash-window and climbed in.

They searched the house, but nothing seemed to be missing, although an upstairs light was on.

They were frying black pudding and tomatoes, when they heard some creaking on the stairs. They seized the trespasser as she tried frantically to open the front door. She fought furiously to free herself, but was of course unequal to the strength of the boys.

They dumped her heaving writhing defiant form on the sofa.

She wore a purple leather coat with a three-inch deep elasticated lilac belt whose large, square, shiny brass clasp consisted of a letter 'U' which hooked up to a letter 'G'. A lavender woollen bobble-hat, scarf and gloves and semi-high-heeled black leather boots completed her outfit.

This had been one of Eleanor's costumes in the film *Ultra-Girl*.

Trapped, she had asked them not to call the police and had laid all the money in her purse – a hundred and sixty pounds – out on a cushion, to pay for the window and for organising its repair.

On Justin's insistence, she showed her driving licence.

'Eleanor Way?'

Breaking and entering, Dennis said, merited being recorded. The police though were too busy dealing with an attack on a speed camera.

'So, what did you intend doing?'

'I thought a Mary Fleet lived here? It was just going to be a gag ... but I've made a mistake. I haven't taken anything.'

They gave her a cup of tea and a large chocolate cookie.

At this point, I arrived and Eleanor, after spilling

some tea into her lap, looked up sheepishly.

On overcoming my astonishment, I asked, 'Did you plan to intercept my letter? And using a forged signature, tell Ellie that I was declining the *rôle*?' I could see no other motive.

She said nothing.

'Is that an *Ultra-Girl* costume?'

She nodded.

'Did Jeanette let you keep it?'

Reluctant perhaps to see herself as wholly in the wrong, she eyed me narrowly. 'So, did you play the "open sesame" card, to win?'

I looked bemused. 'Sorry, what's that?'

She shook her head as if to say, 'Don't come the innocent.'

I cocked an eyebrow and smiled.

Justin found this mildly engaging. 'Do you feel tough and sexy in that get-up?'

She managed a thin smile. 'I liked playing Ceres in *Ultra-Girl* … and I'm bitter over someone I loved … I just like wearing it.' She drank some tea. 'It makes me feel safe, protected.'

Since she tried to resist, the lads gently frog-marched her to the broken window, where I took pictures of her beside it. Then we let her go.

Outside it had begun to drizzle.

At the door, she eyed me fixedly. 'I'm sorry.'

I half-smiled. 'Oh well, "All's well that ends well."'

Inside again, I explained who she was. 'As to rejection, it can hurt I don't doubt, but it's more usual to express it by … being horrible to a subordinate for instance?'

Justin cogitated, but finding no viable alternative, concurred. 'Dressing up to tackle your problems is more escapist, maybe? Also it's a far more titillating or sexual manifestation ... or display.'

Back at home, Sophie sat sipping a glass of wine whilst reading a book.

I flopped into the armchair. 'The cut-throat world of film-making.'

A question mark appeared on her face. 'Il signor Machiavelli ... has he drawn his dagger?'

'Sometimes I wish also I liked wine.' I summarised what had happened.

She gulped more of her trodden grapes. 'Trespass without theft? I doubt it even counts as a crime.'

'A broken window? Damage to property?'

'Pretty small stuff though?'

'I think she imagines herself as a sort of avenger or nemesis in that get-up?'

'I'm not sure it would have struck me as odd? If you're breaking in – climbing over a wall, broken glass, rusty nails – something a bit protective makes sense?'

'But she virtually said that it gave her an ego-trip.'

Sophie was sceptical. 'If I saw four girls dressed like that, I wouldn't think it peculiar.'

Feeling drained, I went to my room.

Jeremiah, that dresser of sycamore trees, saw that when God held someone in derision, his devious plots came to nought.

Eleanor, introspective thwarted and hardened, I foresaw would be changed by some twist of fate.

CHAPTER ELEVEN

On Friday January the fifth, I strolled through a neat and exquisitely tended public garden, supposedly in Berlin.

Wearing a full-length blue dress, a three-quarter lilac suede coat and a very wide hat adorned with yellow flowers and mauve feathers, I tripped on a paving stone and – with a hint of melodrama – fell onto my knees uttering a slightly comical 'Umph.' My basket rolled off to one side. A German army officer on a bench near the band-stand jumped up from reading his newspaper, helped me up and discreetly popped a small bundle of papers into my basket, whilst recovering it. I thanked him inaudibly and continued on my way.

On the seventh, I was in Paris, speaking again inaudibly – as we were at some distance from the camera – to a corporal of the Fourth Hussars in his blue and white number-one uniform, who stood on sentry-go beside a sentry-box at the entrance to the grounds of the French Ministry of Foreign Affairs. Permitted to pass, I walked along a path between two impeccably trimmed lawns towards this stately and renowned two-storey stone building on the Quai d'Orsay.

On the tenth, I was being ushered into an office, supposedly at the Quai d'Orsay, but actually in *Le Théâtre des Italiens*, in Nice.

Under a stuccoed ceiling and on a square of blue carpet stood an oval inlaid desk with an ornate period telephone, a blotter, an ink-well and a scattering of papers and diaries, backed by a large *tricolore* hanging limply from its pole between two sets of French windows.

A solemn French army officer greeted me and we seated ourselves on two Queen-Anne chairs, walnut, with cabriole legs and upholstered with blue hide and brass tacks, one on either side of the desk.

French courtesies preceded factual English phrases and I engaged the bright-eyed Colonel Boulaire of *Le Deuxième Bureau* by smiling coyly and occasionally widening my eyes. Speaking with a fluctuating intonation, I handed him my compact sheaf of papers. 'We believe these are accurate, Colonel.'

He studied them briefly, then nodded deeply.

From a safe he took a green Hessian bag closed at its neck with a purse-string. 'One hundred twenty-franc gold coins.'

'*Merci*.' I took it and rose.

He arose too and shook my hand formally.

These scenes would come in the earlier part of the film. Next, a French frigate would heave to the German freighter with its crooked cargo, but I was not required either in Morocco or aboard ship.

Our film crew were staying in *La jeune bergère*, a fairly posh hotel in Beaulieu-sur-Mer – literally 'Nice-place-by-the-Sea' – and on the third day, I and Antony the locations consultant were superfluous.

As rain rattled against the upstairs lounge windows, we read newspapers, drank coffee and gazed out at the rain-swept quay, where all the tourist cafés had closed for the winter.

'It was good they chose you to play Luise,' he said.

'Oh, thank you.'

'Because you'ld never have hacked the consul's mistress.'

Did I laugh?

'In the Tangier apartment scene, they made the classic error of chloroform on a handkerchief knocking someone out instantly. My father's an anaesthetist and he says it takes three or four minutes. The victim could easily fight back. He says only cyclopropane would do it in one breath.'

On the plane, I sat next to the window and beside two young lasses who worked in a shop.

'Fronting out' I learnt, is a surly stare whilst your tongue makes one of your cheeks bulge. The customer then has either to speak first or to disengage.

I read. 'Plautus adapted a Greek drama, *The Carthaginian*, for the Roman stage. A Phoenician translation existed and he incorporated a few lines into his Latin play. A Roman audience would not understand this, but they were the basis for puns and misunderstandings, so these snippets of Punic verse dialogue have survived ... '

My travelling companions were now discussing party tactics, the prize being a man.

I thought, 'Give a monkey enough shots at a coconut shy and eventually it'll knock one off.'

Yet – whilst tempted to feel superior – I remembered that the coconut I sought was proving distinctly glued to its cup. Where were these golden apples of the Hesperides? When would Prometheus give us his fire?

Back in a humdrum Newcastle, I busied myself catching up with a week of missed lectures.

Sophie had found herself a Japanese boyfriend, Kiyoshi. She seemed to acquire boyfriends in the same way as I might buy a lottery ticket ... and with the same degree of success.

I so wished I also had a boyfriend ... or was I simply in the more receptive or susceptible part of my cycle? I did not wish to be as incurably hardened as Sibylle.

She and I were though quite similar in stature, five foot ten, erect and with small breasts. Also we were not transparently erotic or showy.

Oh Osric, you troubled soul, where are you?

Sophie had made tea. She stared at me.

I nodded.

'Just get him out of your head.'

'I can't.'

'Then let us codename this "Operation Lasso".'

I smiled weakly.

'And may the rope – which currently is woven of invisible psychic fibres – be of sufficient strength?'

'The ox ought to be seeking the noose.'

'Let's hope it knows that?'

Saint Valentine's Day brought its cards.

One said; 'No one loves you; No one wants you; No one needs you.' And inside; 'As much as I do.' I smiled.

One had a barrel of black powder against a castle with a girl on it waving a white flag, a fizzing fuse and a row of coloured kisses. One was just a cluster of prettily drawn abstract flowers. I stood them up wistfully.

Love is a fusion of temporal yearnings with a tingle of the celestial.

In the game of wooing, historically Greek maidens

had danced to the lyre and Renaissance poets had sharpened their quills. All civilisations have had codes of sexual behaviour.

I put this disturbing havoc to one side and bent down over my books. Perhaps I would end up as a nun, innocuous and mum?

Sophie, after only two weeks, was having misgivings about Kiyoshi.

A flat-sounding telephone call one evening, ended as I dished up the corned-beef hash. 'How riveting was that?'

'On a numerical scale, one out of ten.'

'And on an emotional scale?'

She exhaled heavily.

'So, on a par with this useless Welsh potato peeler.'

'It's a question of technique.'

'If you took it to one of those cooking competitions, when the guy said, "One minute to go," you would not even have peeled the spuds.'

Her eyebrows said, 'Do you know what I think?'

'It's like some political ideal; theory untested by practice.'

'All right. I surrender. Given it's no use, shall we refer to it as "he"?'

I gave her a woe-begone smile. 'Nothing we do leads to this mythical sparkling romantic paradise.'

'With Kiyoshi, nothing happens. He has no adult emotions.'

'Oh? But he sleeps here now and then?'

'On the floor. Well once he slept in bed with me, but literally not figuratively.'

'Oh.'

'He is not only incapable of love, but neither is he amenable to it.'

Sophie was only a year older than I, yet there was a touch of that Welsh motherliness about her.

'What about this frolic tonight?'

'No.'

Sophie puffed. 'About your recalcitrant steer, if you leave it too long he will be hurt and then it will be harder to recover.'

I looked at her.

'When my father was a student, I think he had an alcohol problem ... and my mother saved him. Sometimes it is the girl who needs to act.'

I compared Sophie, who ran through quite a few boyfriends yet still seemed quite decent, with Belinda in my Phoenician class, who similarly changed horses every few weeks, yet by contrast looked quite washed-up, hard, promiscuous and sexually grubby. Why the difference? All I could think of was that Sophie was kinder and more sincere, even if it never worked out.

To blot out the unthinkable, I read aloud.

'Greek, though taught at Oxford from 1462, was very basic initially. You had to travel to Padua or Bologna to take it to a higher level ... '

Sophie half-smiled.

'At least we're not like those idlers down the pub ... who intend never to work.'

She sat beside me. We were both unusually down.

'To make life flourish,' she said, 'we have to get this sex thing straight.'

I eyed her.

'Your notions ... need a shrink?'

I frowned. 'A psychiatrist?'

'No. A lessening of your unbounded self-belief.'

'Oh.' I leant back.

She cuddled me. 'No cloying prods? No olive branch? Then if you stubbornly refuse to seek him out, come to this party. I hardly know anyone ... so you'll be someone to fall back on.'

'Thanks,' I muttered sarcastically, then gave her a hug too.

Girls when alone, are more tactile with one another than if men are present.

We changed into more eye-catching clothes. We were two bewitching sparklers, in nice coats and boots, chatting lightly as we wended our way to Spital Tongues.

'So, what happens at this club?'

'It's just a party, but the English Literature Society, so hopefully they're not all two sandwiches short of a picnic.'

'I don't want anything to happen.'

'So, *The Taming of the Screw*?'

'I hope that like Pavlov's dog, the males there are pre-conditioned, so that if I say "no", they'll back off?'

'Then why did you choose that see-through blouse?'

'It's not see-through!' What a tease Sophie was.

It was quite crowded, dimly lit and the floor was carpeted with dark-blue cellular blankets. It had once been rented by nurses and they had pinched them all from the hospital.

Sophie introduced me to Maureen, the one girl she knew, an anorexic, though she held a plate of food.

'We both have small paps,' she said timidly.

'The smaller the sweeter,' I confided. 'Like strawberries, not huge and water-logged.'

Sophie drifted off and an older and very fat guy with curly hair and flabby lips strolled up behind me.

'You have a lovely shaped bottom,' he whispered into my ear.

This was not a good start. I stepped aside. 'That of course, is exactly what I wish to hear.'

'David Fraser.' He offered me a hand which I ignored. 'Marlborough School. Amateur cricketer.'

'Not a high-jumper?' I said tartly, eyeing his huge belly.

He gave me a caustic grin and walked away.

I picked up a cube of Maureen's cheese to pop into her mouth, but she pretended to cough, held my hand back, then took the lump from me. After sinking her front teeth into it, she changed her mind and replaced it on her plate.

Yvonne, whom we had briefly met before, was saying close by, 'George reckons it was his ex-girlfriend who leaked that cosmetics laboratory raid in Rochester.'

'Katy? Yes,' Selena nodded, 'she fancied herself as a leader, a star ... '

'A red giant given her size?'

'Until he dumped her.'

Overhearing this, Maureen took a lipstick from her bag and examined it. 'It says, "ethically tested".'

Choosing to circulate, I went to the drinks table where one Christine mixed a 'Virgin Cuba Libre' for me. 'Cola, rum essence and lime juice.'

'Thank you.'

A plump girl asked for a vodka. 'I'm Denise. Good vodka is tasteless.'

'Then why not drink water?'

She had a doughy expressionless face, clumsy movements and heavy cumbersome breasts. Her genes evidently lacked the 'less is more' coding.

She bared her teeth. 'I wish I had enough money to have them veneered.'

Sophie had captured a thin cheerful raconteur. 'This is Michael and he's *not* a scarecrow, despite appearances.'

'Scarecrows scare birds away,' Michael countered. 'This one has charm, bags of charm.'

'A display?' requested Maureen. 'A teensy sprinkling of bird-seed?'

'There's a snake here who requires charming,' I said, thinking of Fraser, 'though on second thoughts, let's leave him in his pot.'

'But more intriguing than brainless sheep, perhaps?' suggested Yvonne.

'He's a hireling,' I murmured. 'He does not love the sheep.'

Michael said that Tyndale's word for a shepherd's crook was a 'sheephooke'. 'Psalm twenty-three: "The Lorde is my shepherde."'

Yvonne uttered a coarse word. 'Like idiots who believe in angels.'

'We only rarely manifest ourselves,' I confessed.

'Well could you please spread a bit more equality?'

Maureen had studied *Coriolanus*. 'He was scornful of the popular rule and withheld free corn from those who were seditious.'

'I bought some lottery tickets yesterday,' said Michael, 'because I want to be *rich*.'

Yvonne vanished.

I put my oar in. 'If God intends you to win, one ticket is sufficient. It gives Him the means.'

David Fraser, rotating in from the wings where he had been eavesdropping, grumbled about the unpredictability when estimating the odds with girls. 'You can spend fifty quid on one in a club and it's still not guaranteed.'

'What's not guaranteed?' asked Sophie with a straight face.

He exhaled.

'You should lower your sights,' said Michael.

'Considerably,' I supplemented.

Fraser expanded. 'I don't want some straggly-haired witch. I want the *crème de la crème*.' Breathing like a small furnace bellows, he muttered, 'There's an absolute cracker called Sibylle, a German medical student ... '

'We know her,' stated Sophie.

'And the chances of her accepting you would be about the same as the sun not rising tomorrow,' I added.

He glared at me.

I returned a glacial stare. 'Choose an adjective for me; strait-laced, neurotic, perceptive?'

I really would have to ask the palace cook to poison his mushrooms at the next of the Tetrarch's banquets.

His eyes bulged as they rolled up and down my body, then he left and approached Denise, to whom he showed the backs of his chubby fingers. When interlaced, since each of them had a letter tattooed on its knuckle, they spelt 'LETSSHAG'.

'Confucius he say, "Woman with skirts up run faster than man with trousers down,"' whispered Maureen.

'I think we've put him to bed,' I said, not meaning to pun.

Michael said, 'He's in local government. They just feather their own nests. Stuff public service.'

Maureen extended this. 'A criticism of aristocracies is their unequal sharing of wealth, whilst the achievement of socialism is its uniform spread of misery.'

Michael nodded. 'That nails it pretty well.'

We were all quiet for a time.

'If he's just desperate for a screw,' argued Michael, 'why not simply seek the path of least resistance?'

'I think that's what he's doing,' observed Sophie.

She and Michael moved off and I was again alone with Maureen. I pointed to a faint red groove across her nose.

'It's very thin and long, so at night I tie string round my head to try to squeeze it in.'

Initially I was lost for words. 'I'm not sure that gristle can be deformed in that way, but ... you're not unattractive.'

'I wish I had a boyfriend,' she said in a low monotone.

'Well, all any of us can do is behave well, be patient and hope we're rewarded.' As this sounded like my father, I added more cogently, 'And for goodness sake, eat some food!'

I went through a door into the kitchen and found a packet of four blackcurrant tarts on the table.

'Eat one these,' I said sharply.

She took one and looked at it.

'I'll eat one as well. They're not poisonous.' We ate together. 'Hmm, luscious,' I said encouragingly. 'And another?' I squinted my left eye and put my face close to hers. By a second miracle she ate that too and then laughed.

'I wish I had a smiley-face sticker for you.'

She grinned.

'And find something a bit brighter than these black trousers and this chocolate-coloured blouse.'

'Does Sophie have a boyfriend?'

'Umm ... '

'I thought I saw her in Durham, with an older man, on Saturday?'

'No. She was in South Shields then driving a mini-bus for some handicapped children's group.'

'Oh. I wasn't sure.'

Suddenly a great hullabaloo erupted.

Gisela, Yvonne's flat-mate, after repelling one of David Fraser's odious paws from her breast, punched his nose so forcefully that it bled profusely. 'Get off, you filthy swine.'

He glowered at her.

'Go on. Punch me back,' she shouted. 'I dare you?'

Whilst clutching his nose in a handkerchief, he growled, 'I would be delighted ... but I don't want to spend the night in a police cell.'

Everyone here seemed screwed up or at least lacking naturalness; empty-bellied pumas on the prowl in one guise or another.

As Sophie and I walked home, I said, 'Well, that was a high-water mark.'

'All part of life's frayed tapestry, dear.'

'Did you pick up any literary gems?'

'No.'

'Lucky then that you weren't gathering more material for your spy book ... unless it's full of nymphos and Luddites?'

She laughed. 'Mary, don't tell me you're a snob?'

It had underscored for me though, how right it was to love Osric, despite the obstacles.

CHAPTER TWELVE

I had gone incognito to the *première* of *The Moroccan Plot* in Leicester Square. Ellie had sent a ticket at my request.

The scenery shots, especially in Morocco, were superb, but the script was patchy and the acting, good but not outstanding.

In March came the Cinematic Awards shindig in London.

Sophie came down with me and we shared a hotel room.

Getting ready ... where to start? Gold crescent-moon ear-rings? My top-knot of hair ringed by a band of thick gold thread adorned with tiny bunches of brown rubber beads? Dark eye-liner and a dusky deep pink blusher ... just on the cheek bones.

Doing my hair, then my eyebrows ... Sophie says, 'No need to go any lower.'

'Well I wasn't thinking of doing my pubic hair, because that's not likely to be seen whatever happens.'

'Unless some sex maniac tears your dress off?'

The elegant pale orange linen dress had been specially made. It passed under my left arm and over my right shoulder. A huge gold safety-pin and a gold cord round my waist secured it in place. The hem, at mid-calf level, also had been decorated with gold thread. And lastly, gold sandals.

'Cleopatra?' queried Sophie.

'Spot on,' I replied.

'Now all you have to do is to practise some fake smiles to tame the asps.'

I only half-laughed as this would likely be close to the truth.

'And what about that thing round your neck?'

A thin gold chain with a small plain gold cross pendant hung there.

'Are not religious symbols banned?'

'I don't know. Oh, I'll see what happens.'

And so I walked down the red carpet with Jocelyn Swain, he who had played Colonel Marc Boulaire. We were the fifth pair in the entry train for the cast of *The Moroccan Plot*. We were also the fourth film cast to enter. The applause was quite enthusiastic; a mix of politeness and the sense of its being a special occasion no doubt, but perhaps a touch more?

Blonde-haired Chloë was there, three pairs farther back, in a long sage-green dress and gold jewellery.

The *compère* said that we were there to enthrone true gods and goddesses and so by implication, dethrone the false ones. Here he threw a glance at a rival.

I nudged Jocelyn. 'He seems keen on snide remarks. That's the third one so far.'

'I think that's why I like him,' came the whispered reply.

'And this year we have a Peruvian entry. They too have ambitions in the movie industry ... despite having just recruited a director from these islands.' Here he glanced at another enemy.

'Acting should not be over-studied ... in order to seem natural. My own success I owe in part to not reading

The Art of Acting. Someone gave me this "classic" by Professor Oliver Crease, but after two pages, I fortunately mislaid it. The second edition I noted was by Sir Oliver Crease and the third by Lord Oliver Crease. I daresay the next will be by King Oliver Crease. Reputation once established, even if undeserved, tends to be self-perpetuating. Today I hope we will not be dazzled or misled, but be true connoisseurs.'

Latitude Sixty took most of the accolades and it seemed as if *The Moroccan Plot* had lost out until the very final award.

This had the slightly humorous title, *The Garland of Wild Parsley* and that is exactly what it was. Apparently it comes from a ceremony in ancient Argos and those Greeks, those lovers of beauty.

'For the most picturesque actor or actress.'

I was named. I am sure disbelief is often faked, but mine was utterly genuine. Somehow I walked up onto the platform, was kissed by the host. I bowed forwards and this long if frail wreath was hung round my neck by his pretty assistant. It reached down to my navel.

I bowed and smiled to the clapping audience and somehow made it back to my seat.

In the wide reception area to the buffet, stood the photographers.

The heroine from *Latitude Sixty*, Cynthia, with her bay-leaf crown was the star attraction, but I was not without attention. I was happy and I think my smiles were authentic.

Harry Joffe, the editor of *Drama*, wished to interview Cynthia. Her director said, 'Start by saying how indescribably lovely she is. Her mind will then go blank to everything else and you can choose any answers you like to your questions. She will agree unthinkingly and at the end ask, "Do you really think I'm so beautiful?"'

One reporter asked, 'Miss Fleet, apart from an obvious natural talent, to what else do you think you owe your success?'

All I could dredge up was, 'Well I think again, my natural talent?'

He gave a polite laugh.

I soon found myself in a knot of people which included Nick and Jeanette Proctor.

Such events call for a touch of grace and charm, even if much that is said borders on the superficial.

Nick had had past successes and so could afford to be philosophical about his disappointment, but even my single honour salvaged a little for him.

Someone remarked that Cynthia had barely smiled for the photographers. Jeanette, in a *faux* leopard-skin dress with a boot-laced frontal split, said that with those boobs she probably thought no one would look at her face.

With this boorish side-swipe, I could just see her as one of Eleanor's cronies.

I was actually talking with Chloë and trying to juggle a glass of grapefruit juice, a plate and a beef sandwich, when I overheard Jeanette say to Nick, 'And you had better give Eleanor something in this next piece.'

Suddenly – punching well above my weight – I found myself saying, 'Don't you bully Nick or some highly embarrassing pictures of Eleanor might appear.'

She just stared at me.

A softly spoken man in his fifties in a somewhat creased lovat-green suit, took me to one side.

'Terry Duffield. I understand you don't have an agent, Mary?'

'No.'

'Could I take you on? Ten per cent?'

'Er ... well?'

'You're not top-notch, but you're extremely pretty, good-humoured and it seems sensible and open to smaller parts ... which is a saleable bundle.'

I smiled at being called 'a saleable bundle'.

'I'm pretty confident I can find slots for you.'

Not bristling with forced wit or watery promises, I felt him to be trustworthy. I smiled and agreed before returning to the hotel.

This was to be my only big moment in the film world, for unseen events lay just around the corner, but photos of me at the ceremony appeared in five or six film magazines during the coming weeks.

Sophie had spent the day in the British Museum and she seemed quietly happy too.

'How was it?'

I thought for a few seconds. 'Everyone says how magnificent ... or spectacular it is ... but it also resembles sea bathers in January; "Oh the water's lovely. Not freezing at all. Do come and join us."'

We packed up and caught the last train back to Newcastle.

I buckled down to work again and tried – with little success – to push Osric out of my mind.

Two days later, at tea-time, Jocelyn Swain rang the door-bell out of the blue.

Thirty-two, tall and with a façade of sophistication, he raised his hat. 'Mary? I've just been visiting an old school chum locally and thought I'ld "drop by".'

I did not inquire about the almost certainly fictitious 'school chum', but smiled and invited him in.

'Tea?'

'Or shall we go out to dinner ... oh sorry, do you have a boyfriend?'

Sophie walking past in the background raised her brows significantly in my direction.

'Er ... well, yes and no.'

He formed a perplexed expression.

When was Osric going to prove himself and show some courage? 'No, forgive me. It would be lovely. That's very kind.'

He nodded and smiled. 'I am not suggesting anything too serious.'

I smiled too, but thought, 'I bet you are.'

Whilst I made myself presentable, he booked a table at *The Copper Boar* near Morpeth.

Outside he went to recover his Mercedes convertible from Tankerville Place.

As I stood waiting on the kerb, Osric appeared.

'Mary? I was coming to see you.'

'Oh.'

'Are you going somewhere?'

'Er, yes ... I'm sorry ... but do call another day.' I thought there might be some anguish in my voice which he would detect, but did it sound hollow? Might he read it as, 'I've more exciting things to do, but I don't mind stringing you along'? Then Jocelyn pulled up in his flying saucer and I climbed in.

As we drove off northwards, along the Great North Road, I knew I had made a mistake. As the evening air flowed over us, I swore inwardly and it took me much effort not to burst into tears. Why had I not changed my mind?

I was lack-lustre and jittery throughout the meal. I so wanted to see Osric and twice I had to dry a solitary tear.

All I recall is Jocelyn saying that he once sent a Valentine card to some sought-after girl's partner to try to cause a rift.

As he dropped me off in Jesmond, he said, 'I'm sorry. It was a silly mistake on my part.'

I said, 'No, it was a nice gesture ... I'm sorry too.' I ran up the stairs threw myself onto my bed, pressed my face into the pillow and sobbed.

I am unsure if two minutes or twenty minutes went by, but then I felt a hand on the back of my head.

I looked round and saw Sophie kneeling beside me.

'I wasn't sure if I should come in,' she said gently.

I threw my arms round her and sobbed again. 'I love him so much,' I hiccoughed convulsively.

She held me and patted my back. 'Oh dear. You've got it bad ... really bad.'

She made tea and we sat on the sofa.

'I don't know where he lives ... or works ... or else ... '

'I don't know what to do with Kiyoshi,' she began. 'He doesn't seem to show any kindness ... I asked him if he loves me and he says he does … but it's just words.'

I drank some tea with a trembling hand and spilt a few drops on my skirt.

'He's begun to demand sex … but it just isn't right.'

'Even when a couple are more properly together, this business of one partner wanting it more than the other … it's not something anyone talks about, but I daresay it's quite common.'

'It can be misused too. Either one is forced into doing what they do not particularly want to or the other feels blackmailed and humiliated.

Asumi said that Japanese girls do not criticise a boy if he is hurting them. They tolerate it to a certain point, then just leave.'

Later I thought, 'Mary, God is not perverse. Hold firm and do not give up.'

On Wednesday, perhaps because two of my Greek class friends saw I was a bit down, we fixed up a sailing lesson at South Shields.

I drove Imogen, Stella and myself there after lunch and after putting on life-jackets we climbed into a GP 14 dinghy with an instructor named Brian. It was a sunny afternoon and the Tyne estuary though choppy, was sparkling and pale-green and the wind fresh.

In this blue-hulled wooden boat called *Geordie Maid* with its varnished mahogany woodwork and brass cleats and pulleys, we learnt it had a centreboard, a mainsail and a spinnaker. We learnt too of the rudder, wind direction, tacking, ducking under the main boom and then hanging over one side to counter its list.

Gulls squawked and wheeled.

After an hour we seemed to be getting the hang of it when disaster struck.

Whether Brian misjudged the tack as he tried to show off to his 'three popsies' or a freak gust of wind did it, but suddenly the boat heeled right over onto its side and we were all flung into the water. He managed to detach the water-logged sails, but still we could not right the boat even with us all hanging onto its upper gunwale. A launch had to come and rescue us.

We licked ice-creams and padded along the breakwater in squelching sandals to partially dry out in the sun and the breeze before driving back to Newcastle.

Back in the flat, I washed up two mugs and a biscuit plate without giving them any thought and then ate some long-left-over stew from a saucepan on which some wit – probably Sibylle – had stuck a label, 'Culture pot number 1.'

After two hours of Modern Greek, Sophie came in from her Zen class, painting bamboos.

She smiled, more fully than was usual, but said nothing.

'Hullo.'

'The sun is shining,' she whispered mysteriously.

'What? It's just setting.'

'I'm not talking about that ball of burning helium or hydrogen or whatever.'

I waited. 'Then what are you talking about?'

'Aha.' She started to make beans on toast.

I had had enough of this teasing and so refused to try and draw her further.

After adding salt and pepper and stirring the saucepan, she said, 'You've had a visitor.'

My heart raced. 'Who?' I asked as calmly as possible.

'Yes, 'twas he. None other.'

I felt my breathing increase. 'So, what happened?'

She smiled mischievously again. 'I asked him in, gave him a cup of tea and said you wanted to see him … couldn't sleep at night.'

'You didn't bloody well say that, I hope?'

'Well, not the last bit.'

I stood up and grabbed her shoulders. 'Look just be serious. What did you actually say?'

'No, just that. That you would like to see him.'

The toast was burning.

'Oh, damn.'

A thought crossed my mind. I grabbed her shoulders again. 'Did you engineer this?'

'What?'

'His coming here of course.'

'No.'

I looked her hard in the eye. 'I want the truth. If you've lied so far, that's fine. It doesn't matter, but I need to know. Did you somehow contact him and ask him to come?'

'No, I didn't.'

'God's truth?'

'Yes.'

I sighed with relief and flopped back onto the sofa.

CHAPTER THIRTEEN

On Thursday evening, Adrian rang our bell and came in.

'I've seen a chap lately, a few times, looking up at your flat.'

'A prowler?'

'Well, he was stationary.'

'A prowler with an injured leg?'

'Thin?'

'Yes. Look I can't work, do you two want to go and see a film? It's only just turned seven.'

I said, 'I think I need to do some work.'

'The West Jesmond flea-pit cinema had an unusual feature, I'm told,' Adrian divulged *sotto voce*. 'It had double seats on the back row. A pity it closed.'

'Not triples? So which one of us would you have had on your lap?' queried Sophie.

He sucked through his teeth. 'That would have been a tough call.'

We tried not to giggle.

Sophie asked, 'What's on?'

'*Gertie's Dilemma*,' said Adrian.

'God, no,' she spluttered. 'A young high-society Edwardian girl is torn between marrying within her own circle – as is expected of her – and her passion for the local pig farmer's swill-boy. That "dilemma" has been done to death.

The girl, Emilia, walks by a lake, where the swill-hand just happens to be swimming in the nude. Then they copulate in a barn, frenziedly and mind-blowingly.

Love is measured apparently, by the savagery of the act and by its being done with no clothes on. Tenderness or fondness or some underwear would severely lower its score.'

Adrian tried again. 'I think *Ultra-Girl* is being shown again on Screen Two?'

'Oh?' I said, mildly interested.

'It's a bit hack ... a bit fantastic ... three action girls seizing control of an international mining company.'

Adrian sat in the middle. He tried to hold my hand, but I withdrew it.

Charis in a camouflaged combat get-up of mixed greys drove a huge quarry dumper truck over the motorbikes of the thugs hired by her opponents to waylay her.

Zoë Sims in a short skirt and top, abseiled down a cliff using a clamp to grip a blue nylon rope, before paddling a rubber inflatable boat along a river.

Eleanor – as Ceres – in her purple leather coat with its UG belt, sabotaged the brakes under a tycoon's limousine.

It all signalled power and ruthlessness, with a few traces of crude humour dotted here and there. Despite its innovative and engaging antics, it lacked poetry or humanity.

Adrian was good-natured, but I did not intend to encourage anything. I kept my hands in my jacket pockets as we walked home along Saint Mary's Place, but allowed him a brief kiss on the cheek before turning in. Sophie gave him a more intimate cuddle.

Next morning, Felicity – one of Sophie's class-mates – called. Five foot three, a touch petulant and not overly attractive, she none the less had a high opinion of herself.

Eavesdropping – whilst ostensibly reading – I heard Sophie, in between nominally explaining the Japanese pluperfect, probe her about Duncan, her boyfriend.

Afterwards Sophie said, 'Felicity's always looking for a boyfriend richer or more good-looking than the one she's currently with.'

'She might end up with no one.'

'Mr X never quite cuts the mustard.'

'He's probably lucky he's not cutting it.'

'She has some estimable qualities, but is undermined by selfishness.'

'That's the basis of tragedy, isn't it? Someone who is in many ways admirable, is undone by one flaw?'

'Duncan has a good job – he's editor of the socialist journal *The Alternative State* – and he's quite keen on her.'

'From what I overheard, I wondered if she's just neurotic?'

Sophie, tactless and likeable, ended with, 'Then she can just stew in her own juice.'

We went back to our rooms to work.

Love is not a mawkish or incandescent thrill, but a taut irresistible force. It is often cruel and harsh, as it teaches you the stoical arts of suffering and forgiveness.

One late Valentine card, a scene from a wall at Pompeii, showed a girl walking away from the painter. For Petrarch, Laura was – it seems – a girl he only saw from afar, yet who affected him for the rest of his life. Her chaste image inspired him to adore her and thus to conquer the lesser side of his physical nature.

That afternoon, I lay down for a little nap and as I dozed, I dreamt of Joseph's sheaf of corn and of those of his brothers bowing down to it.

My sheaf stood upright. Others deferred. 'If I am putting myself on a high hill, it is because my self-esteem is not misplaced.'

I kissed the pillow, full of cut-up pieces of old cloth and whispered, 'Osric my love, I want you to hold me ... and I want you inside me.'

CHAPTER FOURTEEN

On the Friday evening, Sophie was off to another party.

'Do you want to change your mind and come?'

'No. I'm floundering with this pesky Phoenician.'

She shook her head. 'He won't try again.'

'Maybe not,' I conceded, yet my intuition told me otherwise.

Mary from Magdala had played perilous and knife-edge games in and around Herod's court, yet had been guided – or guarded – by the steadfastness of God.

Sophie reappeared. She had reverted to the black leather mini-skirt, the frilly low-cut white blouse and the dabbing on of too much purply-coloured make-up.

She sat beside me. 'Mary, even if someone is the right guy, things need a push. You cannot just sit there and refuse to do anything? And I noted down his address for you.'

I gave her a hug. 'Sophie, I know you mean well ... and I'm grateful ... but I have to heed my instincts.'

She gave me a sad yet kindly smile, patted me on the head and set off.

Our sitting-room faced the road, though a hedge separated the front garden from the street. I left a light on and the curtains open and retired to my own room with a cup of tea. Our sitting-room and Sophie's room were at the front, whilst mine and the bathroom were at the back.

I opened the book of Phoenician grammar, but a lowly form of contemplation seemed more essential. I knew that tonight something had to happen. I felt a low-grade anguish, an adumbration perhaps of the agonies in Gethsemane. I fell onto my knees. Ought I to dislike myself more and be less critical of others? Ought I to know my own worthlessness and to be helpful to Osric?

We are alone in our decisions. I read Psalm thirty-nine. 'For I am a stranger with you, a sojourner like my forefathers. Look away from me, that I may know of gladness, before I depart and am no more.'

Could conceit have been another of Mary's seven sins? And pride yet another? Pride in her conquests? Pride in her body's physical allure?

If there are say 'x' desirable human qualities, no one will possess all of them. I had integrity but was perhaps inwardly – though not outwardly – ungenerous. But such characteristics are hard to pin down; the spectrum broad.

A church clock had chimed nine and Osric had not come. Sophie had given him some encouragement and I had trusted his not being so petty as to be jealous or sulky over that stupid outing with Jocelyn Swain.

I made cheese on toast, then, as I started to close the curtains, I jumped. Osric stood on the far pavement, looking up.

I slid up the window and waved.

I let him in and we climbed the stairs. 'Sophie said you called on Wednesday. I should have been in, but three of us went to South Shields for a sailing lesson and the boat capsized.'

I closed the curtains, made tea and turned the lights down.

I sat him on the sofa, put down the mugs of tea and cut my slice of cheese on toast in half. Also sat on the sofa, I put my hand down near to him so that he might take it.

My heart quivered ... but I hid it.

He looked at me. His eyes said simply, 'I love you Mary,' but his tongue said, 'Who was the big fish in the Mercedes?'

'Do you mean that tiddler?' I tutted and shook my head. 'You must have been using your magnifying glass?'

Reassured, he smiled.

He looked nervously at my hand and trembled.

I said, 'Don't be so panicky,' then I turned and put my arms round him loosely. We kissed, pressed our heads together side by side and then looked at one another closely.

Forgetting the tea and the cheese on toast, I took him through into my bedroom where I sat him on the bed and then knelt down in front of him and held his hands.

'Meeting you has been the most momentous event in my life.'

'Shhh. Don't say that,' I admonished him. 'You'll upset the spell.' I smiled. 'What's that blob of make-up on your cheek?'

'It must have come off you.'

'Oh, that's my daft flat-mate again.'

Then we were on the bed, kissing and cuddling gently yet zealously, a desire too long withheld.

After a while, we went to drink the tepid tea and eat the cold cheese on toast, before going to bed.

The next morning being a Saturday, the engineering

works where he was employed, worked until midday, so Osric left to catch the Metro at seven and I promised to pick him up from his work at twelve.

I observed the cover of my Phoenician book, distorted through my tears. I wept with joy and gratitude.

The door-bell seemed to play a key part in my life at Newcastle and at ten past ten it rang.

This time is was a deputy features editor from a Sunday newspaper magazine.

Dawn Mort – or Sandy as she styled herself – wore a calf-length, tight, yet shapeless dress, a fake fur jacket, a long string of wooden beads which she frequently fingered like a rosary and a gross excess of make-up. She flashed her I.D. card.

I sat her down and made tea.

'We are hoping you might be able to help us with an article?'

'Oh?'

'About the film director Nick Yates?'

'Oh yes?'

'You've worked with him, I understand?'

'That's so. Easy to work with and pleasant.'

This last phrase clearly did not hit the right button.

Smiles seemed to be a large part of her armoury. 'He has been accused of sexual impropriety by a number of actors.'

'Do you mean "actresses"?'

'We cannot use that word any more, but yes, female actors.'

'Who says we can't say "actresses"?'

'Well it's not gender neutral.'

'Well it's not meant to be.'

'Well never mind that. Let's move on.' More bead-fiddling was followed by, 'Did you yourself experience any sexual coercion ... did he ask for sexual favours in exchange for positive outcomes to auditions, for instance?'

'No. Absolutely not. He was always perfectly straight with me.'

'We are prepared to offer good money for the "right" material?'

'Are you suggesting I lie?'

'He has been implicated by three other female actors ... and of course now this very weird sex game has come to light?'

I had not heard of this, but decided not to ask. 'So I would only be adding slightly to an already tarnished reputation?'

'Precisely.'

'Well he behaved decently to me and if that doesn't interest you, then good-bye.'

She stood up, holding her thin document case. 'Oh well, if you can afford to throw away 10K?'

'So you thought I would fold, for money? That's quite an insult.'

She shrugged. 'It must be nice to be one of those London plutocrats?'

'London?' As I ushered her to the top of the stairs, I swapped to a West Country burr. 'No-i. Oi comes from a far-rm, in Devon, oi.'

Half-way down, she stumbled and as her dress prevented her moving one foot far from the other, also fell, though did not break a bone. She gathered herself up slowly, in much agony and with a cut on her hand and a rent in her jacket. She would no doubt have bruises as well.

'I'll sue you,' she bellowed. 'This handrail's loose ... that's against health and safety.'

'Oh, piss off.'

Off she hobbled.

I set off for North Shields, stopping to buy bundles of fire-wood, matches, beans, sausages, bread, bottled coffee, juice and biscuits.

I drew into the yard at Shiel's Boilers and Engineering Limited.

Osric's boss eyed me. 'Hullo?'

'Hullo. I'm Mary. I've come to collect Osric.' I smiled.

He looked at me with a degree of disbelief.

Osric appeared from the workshop, rubbing his hands on some cotton-waste.

'Is *this* your girlfriend?'

'It is,' came the stout reply.

'How did you manage that?'

'What?'

'You have hidden abilities my lad.'

I tried to look bashful.

Claude beckoned me into a large tin-roofed shed and showed me the old six-wheeled lorry they were restoring. It had been found rusting on some estate and looked to me so skeletal in parts as to be beyond repair.

'It's a 1937 Albion "R". It'll take us a year, but you can come along with us when we return it. We'll all dress up in period clothes.'

'Aren't these mudguards too far gone?' They seemed to be just ribs and paper-thin corroded metal.

'No. We'll take them off, sand-blast them and then build them up with a lead alloy compound. Be like new.'

'Who's paying to have this done?'

'A Mr Marshall. He's in his fifties, saw it, fell in love with it and took out a new fifty-thousand-pound mortgage on his house to pay for it.'

I was impressed. 'That's real love.'

'Mostly we repair older machinery … often making spare parts which cannot be found anymore.'

I noted a large lathe, a power hack-saw and piles of shiny swarf.

It was one week before the Easter holidays and Osric and I drove to Kielder Forest, where we picnicked beside the reservoir. We found some rocks to place round the fire and I had brought a frying-pan along.

Dusk descended and a light breeze blew off the water, but the fire made it romantic. And more than that, I was so happy.

I knew he liked working with machinery, so I asked, 'Why did you apply for a general arts degree if your aptitude – and love – is for engineering and metalwork?'

'I liked Latin at school and thought that with pure maths and some history, it would give a broader background. Leaving home is about taking chances … and being prepared to accept the outcome.'

The darkness increased and the lake was still. We had eaten our sausages and beans.

On an old shepherd's tartan plaid, we lay and talked and kissed and cuddled.

Osric had quite an introverted mind, making it difficult – unless someone loved him – to attune themselves to his leaps of thought. He also was seldom witty, but life is nor primarily about rolling in the aisles.

He came from Maryport on the Cumbrian Coast and knew much about the history of railways, especially the Furness Railway.

We held one another tightly and I pulled our coats over us to keep us just warm enough.

'I so love railways ... especially bridges. When I was three, I saw my first train – an engine and three wagons on a branch line crossing a small girder bridge with stone abutments ... and knew immediately, that it was something wonderful and special.'

After we had kissed many, many times, I stroked his hair and asked, 'In the summer, shall we go on a holiday somewhere? Somewhere where there's a railway?'

How delightful were his caresses. Without them the door could open to pain, to being wanton, to temptation, to doing dodgy things; perhaps to becoming another Eleanor?

We slept on and off whilst the stars – and the angels – kept a silent watch.

CHAPTER FIFTEEN

The fee from *The Moroccan Plot* cleared a half of the Glenthorn Road mortgage, whilst still leaving a reserve for the summer holidays.

I also gave sporadically to the homeless and to the Salvation Army.

Terry Duffield rang. 'Mary, short notice. Can you do a thirty-second non-speaking part this Thursday?'

The film was *The Xenon Nebula*.

Lord Sun-Hover-Beech seems to have lost all emotional reaction. In a psychiatric clinic, rigged up to an electro-encephalograph, dozens of sensors all pinned to his scalp are wired up to a computer. He is asked about his wife, his castle and its treasures; pictures of cute puppies are shown to him; some Bach is played. The display remains blank. No dots representing different parts of his brain light up. Then I breeze in, a slinky young nurse wearing a blue short-sleeve uniform dress, a short apron and a white cardboard hat with a red cross on it and suddenly his electronic brain image starts twinkling all over, like a Christmas tree.

Ellie rang. Nick was asking me to do a one-scene, non-speaking slot in the film *A Tuscan Conspiracy*.

In Elstree, Nick seemed fraught. The press were giving him a rough ride. Of the cats let out of bags, many he protested, were phantom moggies. 'And even the real ones have grown extra fur.'

I sympathised.

'Eleanor and that snake Meryl Umboko rigged

this forest bridle-way hoax ... but thank you for your loyalty, Mary.' He swigged his coffee. 'Now, in *A Tuscan Conspiracy* you're Arianna, a librarian in Pisa. That scene's listed for June the second. If it clashes with your exams, let us know ... and quickly.'

When you start to be known and are known to be reliable, such crumbs as these are offered without an audition.

Chloë rolled up and kissed both Nick and myself with unaffected spontaneity.

After Nick had expounded her *rôle* to her, she and I went to an Italian restaurant.

'Do you have a boyfriend, Mary?'

'Yes. He's called Osric.' I hinted at our wobbly start.

Chloë too felt herself to be drawn to a very hesitant lad. 'My friend says that his not answering the message I sent, is his answer, but ... he might just be shy?'

'What's his name?'

'Alwyn.'

'Don't give up too quickly.'

She smiled. 'You're the only one who's said that.' A twinge of unhappiness infected her voice.

The cannelloni arrived.

'So, what's this "weird sex game", Nick's being accused of?'

'Eleanor's says – in some glossy magazine – that he pulled her to the ground in a wood, amid some bluebells and then – as they struggled – had an orgasm whilst lying across her.'

'Across her? At ninety degrees?'

'Well ... at some acute angle. She was wearing her *Ultra-Girl* leather get-up.'

'But bluebells don't flower until summer?'

'Perhaps they weren't in bloom.'

I shook the grated Parmesan canister over my food. 'Anyway, she's lying on the ground in a wood?'

'Supposedly he had asked her to his house ... but it is then she – it seems – who persuaded him to go for a walk in the nearby woodland. She trips up on a tree root, he stoops down to help her up, she pulls him down on top of her and someone just happens to be there with a camera.'

I puckered my brow. 'That all sounds pretty improbable?'

'Yet it seems to be the best fit.'

We began eating.

'And apart from this "angle", is her coat undone?'

'She says he didn't penetrate her, because in his frenzy, he released himself prematurely.'

'Sorry to be picayune, but none of this adds up. What about his supposed impotence?'

'Which is why it's obviously a set-up.'

I tilted my brows inwards. 'Isn't this libellous?'

'Unless she then did stuff and there's at least a smear on her coat?'

I refilled our glasses, mine with spring water, Chloë's from the carafe of white Chianti. 'And her motive? Revenge for being side-lined? Money?'

'A woman spurned? Or spermed?'

'And it's given her an extra splurge of publicity I suppose?'

'A splurge of something.'

I tried not to smile.

'What's so unfair,' said Chloë, 'is that no one dreams of blaming her. He's the monster.'

'Hmm … but aside from this event, do you think she's suffering from some form of chronic psychosis?'

'I don't understand such things … but what do you make of girls who like wearing leather?'

'Do you mean to excite male interest?'

'Or for any reason?'

'It's hard to say. Whoever the wearer is, her thoughts will be her own … so it's individual.'

'Hmm.'

'In most cases though, it'll just be fashion or its appeal factor. You do see a neatly shaped, tapered leather coat or a nicely cut pinafore dress with attractive stitching … but a lot of this stuff just looks rough or common.'

'It tends to stretch too and go out of shape.'

We ordered some desserts.

'I had a boyfriend who wanted me to buy a leather coat, a black one with a belt and a nice glint to it. His eyes just lit up and he tussled and rolled me around like a nut-case.' She gave an arch smile.

I smiled too. 'It's unfathomable, isn't it?'

'Yet – to state the obvious – it's showy and it makes us look a bit defiant and hard-to-get.'

'A magic wand?'

A week later Nick walked into the sea and drowned. *A Tuscan Conspiracy* was cancelled.

Osric often spent the night at the flat in Otterburn Terrace.

He asked about the art of acting; flow, suppleness, techniques of emphasis.

'There are points to learn, but it mustn't confuse …
like the centipede, who when asked how he walked,
grew so muddled that he fell over.

Daddy – whom you must meet soon – adheres to
notions of simplicity. He thinks that if you believe that
behind the world's colourful scenery, there are no nasty
trolls, then if they are there, they will be deactivated.'

'Deceit always dumbfounded my grandfather.'

'Amongst students, it's sincerity or honesty which
cause shock.'

'This paternal grandfather, I always felt that his
honesty somehow protected him.

He fought in Burma in World War Two and once,
going out with a patrol to a village where they were
suffering from malnutrition, someone suggested taking
along a couple of sacks of rice. The quartermaster said
they could if they wished, but it would not really make
any difference. I forget whether they did or didn't, but
the mere fact that they thought of it shows a degree of
humanity.'

I tried to imagine the scene, dwellings made of
bamboo and woven strips of leaf in a lush dense humid
jungle, with leeches, flies and mosquitoes.

We were lying on my bed, kissing and cuddling on
and off whilst talking.

'On that Burma-Siam railway, there is a very deep
cutting. The Japanese were in a hurry and with a tunnel
only a few would be able to work in the confined space,
whereas with a cutting hundreds or even thousands
could be digging at once.'

'Your grandfather wasn't a prisoner-of-war?'

'No.'

'Does that railway still exist?'

'A part of it does. Old servicemen take holidays to travel on it.'

'Shall we go there in the summer? Are you due some holiday?'

'Nine or ten days ... but it would be too expensive.'

'I can pay for it my sweet.' I stroked his hair. 'I'm to receive three thousand pounds for a cancelled film appearance.' It must have seemed so disproportionate to what he earnt.

'Three thousand pounds? For doing nothing?'

'Well, the audition was tough.'

'With your looks? Anyway, I thought you said there wasn't an audition?'

'Well, dealing with the adders and back-stabbers. That's *really* tricky.'

We kissed ardently and rolled around for a time, then stood up, straightened out our clothes and went through to the sitting-room where Sophie was sitting.

'My father saw Jains in India, sweeping the path gently before them so as not to tread on any living creature. He was very struck by their holiness and their self-abnegation.'

I emptied two tins of cock-a-leekie soup into a saucepan.

Sophie waved a hand at a thin monograph on Giotto. 'A footnote in history?'

I shook my head. 'It's about the paints used in Renaissance art.'

'Asumi's grandfather was a Zen swordsman. That too

requires the subjugation of "self", in order to become a master ... to submit to the "it".'

Osric told of a Japanese soldier captured by his grandfather's platoon. 'This was most unusual. Perhaps he had fallen asleep? After some weeks, he began to talk and said that because his wife had wept on the quayside as his ship left Yokohama, he wanted to die in battle. That's so hard for us to comprehend.'

Sophie replied, 'So his combat tactics were about as feeble as yours?'

'What?'

'For wooing Mary? One of your rivals at least nicked her cardigan, then brought it round saying he'd found it.'

I suddenly remembered the cushion, but of course that was the café's, not mine. I had only sat on it.

Sophie seemed ill at ease, so I asked if she were all right.

She looked up at the ceiling, then lanced the boil. 'This Japanese,' she said hesitantly, 'it's not that I made a mistake, but now I want to do something else.'

I sat down beside her. 'Don't worry. These things are never wasted.'

'I want to read ancient Greek.'

'As in Homer?'

'Yes, but you need to start with classical Greek.'

'Definitely. They're not so different. Some of the noun endings are... and of course it's poetry; dactyls I think.'

'There's something so profound about that era.'

Osric whilst dishing up the soup, said, '"Forfeit be thy life for thy profanity," is more colourful than "Where's the bathroom?"'

'But what could you do with it?'

'Didn't I ask you that about Phoenician?'

'So you might switch to general arts ... like me?'

'It sounds crazy ... but it's what I want.'

I gave her a hug.

The soup brought us all together in a huddle.

'I went to an extramural lecture on Homer and Hesiod,' she confided, after one spoonful. 'Homer is about heroes, vividly painted shields, bronze spears and gold breastplates, whereas Hesiod's peasants are working narrow strips of land with poor wooden ploughs, wearing unadorned clothing and eating unvaried and scanty food ... but although we usually regard the heroic figures as the more exalted, everyone has significance and is not without their sources of reward or gifts of imagination or craftsmanship. Each has enough to evoke their curiosity and to fill up their days.'

I printed off a picture of a northern Thai railway station; a cream and brown wooden structure with a wide roof, a flag-pole and flower troughs, simple but neat and well-cared-for. The stone platform was low, the rails gleamed.

As Osric had to work, I went to Nick's funeral alone.

A thin turn-out of film buffs and former colleagues sat behind two rows of family and relatives. It was a dreary affair.

Chloë arrived late. At the reception afterwards, she and I found ourselves talking to an M.P.

Graham Foy was divorced, pleasant in a rather prescribed way and perhaps more attentive to Chloë than he wished to advertise.

'We're fledgeling actresses,' Chloë explained.

'With the most appealing plumage.'

'An orchestra my father often conducts, often gains sponsors with the help of Ponsford Manley M.P., who's rumoured to have had a Stasi controller before the collapse of the old East Germany. How true are such things?'

Foy looked into her pale-grey eyes and smiled gently. 'If an M.P. shows sympathy for a non-aligned country, they may invite him there as a guest and later someone in their embassy here will send him articles or ask him to speak at a dinner. Now in the case of East Germany, such an official would probably have been a Stasi officer, but he would not control the M.P. in the same way that he would a spy.'

Sensing some magnetism between them, I went off to say a few complimentary words about Nick to his wife. She though was under no illusions and – as I quickly learnt – was inured to any soft soap.

Sophie arranged her switch from Japanese with honours to become in September a second-year general arts student. I would then be starting my third year.

The Thailand trip was what one might dub 'an experience'.

Our delayed flight into Bangkok meant that we reached the hotel just before midnight. Only its deserted bar, intended for a German clientele, was open. We sat in this fake medieval tavern, backed by polystyrene 'oak' beams and stone-effect wallpaper and were served coffee with amoretti by a Mongolian-looking girl in a Bavarian dirndl and a blonde wig. The table-mats depicted an early Japanese iron-clad warship and the background music was *Little Boxes on the Hillside*.

The buffet breakfast was a scramble, watched by an immobile, corrupt-looking *maître d'hôtel*, wearing a heavy gold neck-chain and a *Madonna* T-shirt.

We visited the highly ornamental Grand Palace and looked at a spotless sun-reflecting gilded Buddha, which unlike the usual ponderous pot-bellied variety, was lithe, feminine and with a slender neck and arms and given that she leant forwards, if painted in varied colours, could have stood in as a figure-head on an old wooden sailing ship.

A shrine built of heavy red, orange and black beams with a bowed bronze-tiled roof was attractive, but neither Osric nor I felt any affinity for this alien civilisation. A Sri Lankan tourist took a photo for us as we linked arms before an unknown carved wooden god.

We caught a train to Kan Chana Buri by the skin of our teeth, tumbling with our rucksacks into a third-class carriage as it was moving. Three goats instead of nibbling a box of odd-looking vegetables, preferred my short trousers. It was crowded, there was no trolley service or toilets and no corridor connection to the first-class section.

Our delight though was simply holding one another and being together. The tea plantations, the green-gold-lit paddy fields and native villages were – though scenic – mere fleeting artefacts.

After a night at a more tranquil hotel beside the River Kwai, we took the train which crosses the bridge then winds its way for forty miles between the pale-green, gently swirling 'Little Kwai' and some sheer cliffs to Nam Tok, the end of the line. Here it rained, although it was not yet the monsoon season. We bought a red and an orange parasol and used them as umbrellas as we took the short walk to an unimpressive waterfall. The terrain was hilly and the vegetation looked thick and inhospitable.

An elderly Scot told us that his father – who had worked on the railway as a prisoner-of-war – had come home very frail and had needed to swig dilute hydrochloric acid with his meals to aid his digestion.

'In the fifties, a Japanese team sent to Britain to see how we ran our welfare set-up, by a fluke turned up at his office and he greeted them in Japanese, before explaining that he had recently given them a hand building a railway. They were most apologetic, so my father received an apology, even if no one else has.'

The weather was sultry though not excessively hot and luckily the number of tourists was bearable. The train consisted of semi-open carriages pulled by a Bo-Bo diesel-electric engine, so Osric tells me. The famous and original River Kwai bridge had apparently been farther to the south.

'The torque of a squirrel-cage motor is maximum when not rotating, as opposed to an internal combustion engine where torque is zero when not rotating, hence the need for a clutch.'

I smiled. I think I understood this.

For dinner we ate a milder 'yellow' curry with some Verdi arias playing in the background, half-way between Wagner and West End musicals, I suppose?

Next morning we hired a jeep. Osric did not drive and I lacked the required international driving licence permit. A long stiff oily grin from the car rental guy seemed to indicate an impasse, until I realised that his array of blue, green, black and yellow teeth might mean that he was open to a bribe? And so it proved.

He tried hard to recommend an 'attraction' where elephants load logs onto railway wagons. I guessed that another family member owned this 'attraction'.

We drove a hundred miles northwards, into hillier rougher terrain, wilder and only cultivated in patches.

After a night in a tourist cabin on stilts at Umphang, we set off next morning on the two-day 'Rain and Shine Jungle Mini-Trek'.

Having mild tummy upsets, we had bought a bunch of green bananas, which supposedly would help to calm our insides. Whilst we sorted out our stuff in the back of the jeep, a monkey nipped through the open passenger door and stole them. Being nineteen too, lacking the correct kit did not bother us. 'It'll be all right,' we agreed.

We strode along behind a guide and eight other 'adventurers', through tall undergrowth and beneath a high canopy of trees. Our shoes and socks were solid enough, but our cropped trousers left our lower legs exposed. The other trekkers wore long trousers tucked into their socks. We did not tread on any snakes or scorpions, but their lesser brethren – invisible but with large jaws – feasted on our bare calves. Some tiny birds – red-throated green ones and black and yellow tit-like ones – flitted about.

After some vegetable stew beside a camp fire, we were told that the tree-houses, fifty feet above us, were our sleeping quarters.

We craned our necks and stuttered.

'You cannot sleep on the ground,' said the guide, 'because of the snakes. Cobras, Malaysian blue corals, many species of pit viper – green, cardamom, white-lipped, Pope's, Eastern Russell's ... '

I seized Osric and the swaying rope ladder with more confidence than I felt. Luckily there was no wind but it was hard to sleep in this makeshift box nailed onto two branches of what I guess was a huge teak. There were eerie squawks and shrieks all night and our single blanket was prickly.

I said, 'Perhaps one day we shall laugh at this.'

In the morning with improved tummies but still balloon-like ankles, we rafted down a smooth-flowing river with a few baby cataracts, then hiked back to the car park.

Next day we drove south to a town with a floating market.

Its picturesque narrow boats with pointed prows and sterns – and crammed with boxes of fruit, utility items, straw hats, coolie hats and bags with elephant cut-outs sewn on them – were moored four abreast on the river.

Like true xenophobes, we bought hamburgers and cola and ate sat in a moored boat, which rocked pleasingly on the cool grey-green water.

During the early evening, driving back to Kan Chana Buri, I sensed a dip in our nearness and so stopped the jeep on the edge of the village of Khao Ban. Did Osric feel upstaged? His family were quite poor. I was paying. I was driving. I took hold of his hands and asked, 'Osric, you do love me don't you?'

'Of course I do,' he replied holding my face in his hands whilst his eyes moistened.

Over the hills crept the first hints of dusk.

'Before the moon and the stars, I want only one thing … not travelling to all the corners of the earth – trying to fill some mental void – but being with you.'

He looked at me. 'I'm sorry. You're so pretty, so able … '

'Remember *Hamlet*, "To thine own self be true".'

He pondered this.

'I cannot speak one word of this language and I dislike being in a country where I cannot say at least a few basics.'

Despite the awkwardness in this cramped vehicle, we cuddled one another.

'Back to that "To thine own self be true"? It's spoken by Polonius, who's a shifty courtier?'

'Yes, but I think it holds good, none the less? It's a bit on the same turf as the Delphic oracle's "Know thyself." We should not strive to be the king of the castle, nor to abase ourselves, but just to allow our natures to find that which God wishes to bestow on us.'

'You speak Italian? You must read some Petrarch to me when we're back.'

'It'll be in the old Tuscan dialect and it's poetry, but I think it's still close enough to modern Italian?'

The name of my senior school had recently been changed from 'grammar' to 'academy'. No doubt the former had sounded too élitist.

'At school, a lad who was quite poor at Latin, used to make up sentences, usually with duff grammar, yet with an infectious humour. He said, for instance, to my friend Ruth, *"Veni in cubiculum"* – "Come into the bedroom" – and howled with laughter.'

'And did she?'

'Of course ... *not.* Enthusiasm's the elixir of life. Brilliance is overrated. Honesty is the essential yardstick; money over-glorified.'

'But we need to earn a wage ... and the unorthodox rarely qualifies.'

He stroked my back and my hair and we were silent for a time. 'I first saw you walking into the Percy Building on Monday the third of October ... six days after we had started our courses. I have revisited that doorway, like some sacred site, now and then ... especially when sad.'

I said nothing.

'Will you marry me?'

My head was hanging down over his lap. A smile – invisible to him – formed on my features. I pinched his tummy and said softly, 'Yes.'

He lifted me up and we kissed and cried for a time. I said, 'I love you ... and I know that it will never go away.'

As we drew near to Kan Chana Buri, we saw in the last rays of the twilight, a man lying beside the road. I braked.

'He might be one of those methamphetamine addicts.'

'Perhaps, yet I have a feeling.'

He was a Sri Lankan tourist, a middle-aged man, not unlike the one who had taken our picture for us at the shrine in Bangkok. He had been beaten and robbed.

He seemed to be unconscious, but when he realised we meant no harm, opened his eyes. He had simply been playing possum to avoid another beating.

A head wound had bled copiously and he was still dizzy.

In the town we bought some antiseptic tinctures and some bandages for him, paid for a room for the night in our hotel and gave him enough money to reach his consulate in Bangkok on the morrow.

There was no way he could properly thank us, but he said, 'At home I have been robbed too, though not physically ... by tax officials. When the British ruled, the administration was honest. Now it is utterly corrupt.'

In our own room, I said, 'As in the parable of the Good Samaritan in Luke's gospel, sometimes someone whom you do not know, who owes you nothing and can expect nothing in return will help you out of a sticky spot.'

'Perhaps so.'

'And it's surprising how often it happens?'

Osric gave an ironic grin. 'Perhaps you're luckier than I am?'

'And *vice versa*. Someone you know well and is indebted to you, plunges the knife in.'

Osric grinned. 'Are we thinking of schoolgirls?'

I grinned too. 'Whatever makes you think that?'

Next morning we took the train back to Bangkok.

Ko-Ko's Bazaar sold antiques, a few of them genuine. A large silver coin dotted with ideographs, battered and worn enough to be authentic, said on its label; 'Circa 1730'.

'Bicarbonate of soda for twenty minutes, brush it with a toothbrush and it might come up cleaner and clearer,' mused Osric. 'But then it has no meaning for us. We can't decipher it.'

A pair of rings, gold, thickish, irregular, had each a notch with a tiny stone in it, one blue and one pink. 'Nineteen-seventies? And Scandinavian going by their design?'

They fitted our fourth fingers and we bought them as engagement rings.

On the plane, before lights out, we were served coffee and cherry cake.

'Stuff those curries ... and those temples. Give me Jesmond or Tynemouth any day.' I took his hand. 'Our next trip, my loved one? Kielder Forest again or the Cumbrian Coast?'

'Or Devon?'

CHAPTER SIXTEEN

Mummy and Daddy could not have been nicer to my fiancé, which was good or else I would have let them know.

'The return of the prodigal daughter?' mused Daddy.

'And why prodigal?'

'Because sometimes you need a prod. Osric, how are you finding our prodigal daughter?'

'Very prodigal, so far.'

Daddy laughed, though I could see he was unsure how to interpret this. I think Mummy was more sure.

'There's a special service at Saint Colomb's,' Daddy said. 'I promised Gemma LeCocq that we would go, but afterwards we'll go out to dinner.'

As she climbed into the pulpit with her one-centimetre bristle of hair and a hint of large biceps, I whispered to Daddy, 'I bet she uses the word "Lesbian".'

'Oh don't be ridiculous,' he muttered.

Four sentences into her sermon, I was proved right. I jabbed him in the ribs with my elbow.

Then she moved onto the serious business of scrapping our Trident missile submarines; the lotus-eaters, the dreamers of pink elephants, of sacred blue-hot knob-sized brickbats which would certainly bounce back. Odd squeaks started to come out of the organ.

Courage and defending your patch, contests and deterrence just are an innate element of the human condition. Anyone with half a brain-cell can see that.

The reading was from Ephesians, chapter six: 'Put on the full armour of God … '

The young girl who said the prayers, asked, 'Please God, give everyone in heaven nice pictures to draw.' I thought it so delightfully other-worldly ... a haven of purity and unsullied light.

Spiritual battles are deep down beneath the mould, the ones with the demons or deceivers which lead us into dark caverns. Prayer should not be about wishing for some never-never-land.

As we left, LeCocq gave me an ambiguous grin. 'I trust you're well, Mary?'

'Yes thank you, Gemma.' I hoped she was not ogling my bum.

The dinner was in a comfy homely pub with a low-beamed ceiling and the banter congenial and unfettered.

'The brightest member at Saint Colomb's,' said Mummy, 'is Howard, the lay reader, but it's rare anyone listens to him.'

'I can sympathise with that,' remarked Daddy waggishly.

'An example?' asked Osric.

'Well,' Mummy began, 'last Easter he compared supplicants and psychopaths. Psychopaths lack insight. He told of a psychology lecturer who ran a test with his class to determine the spread of their emotional responses. The results showed an outlier, a psychopath in the group. It was himself.

Supplicants, though self-centred, do recognise it.'

'One clue,' continued Daddy, 'is that a psychopath will be after something. At a party, you will chat amiably with him and not be too worried about where it's heading, but he will be trying to steer it to some objective.'

'They're after something emotional or material?' asked Osric.

'Either.'

'There's a lot of it about,' I said.

'This place has a nice softly-lit cosy atmosphere,' said Mummy. 'I tried to book a table at *The Crow*, but it was hosting a "Whodunnit" evening.'

'What happens at those?' I asked.

'Uncle Basil's been to two or three. You sit six to a table, the scene is set and a master-of-ceremonies hands out cards with clues and during the meal various incidents or extra clues occur, until at the end each table makes a best guess as to the villain.'

'Is it fun?'

'Basil and Marlene seem to think so … but it might depend on your table companions?'

I had been mildly irritated by LeCocq's depiction of Luke the evangelist. He had propounded the Good News as not just for the Jews, but for everyone, but she had to add to the 'everyone', 'regardless of social position, skin colour, creed, sexual orientation, blah, blah, blah,' like some automatic recording. 'Everyone' is 'everyone'.

I said to Daddy, 'She's implying that we – her audience – are narrow-minded and with prejudices which need to be curbed.'

'Don't say anything, for goodness sake. Besides we do have to steer a course between traditionalism and modern thinking. For the Puritans of the Civil War era say … Cromwell, Milton … ninety per cent of their reading would have been the Bible. An odd news-sheet perhaps, a book on fishing once in a while … '

'With the Restoration came the first coffee-houses, bawdy plays, convivial discourse … but there was originality there. LeCocq is just reiterating propaganda.'

Yet the candles were delightful, the crab on toast with some herby butter, the Chateaubriand with red cabbage and the *crème brûlée* all perfect and I was so grateful it all went off calmly and happily.

As we left, a quite lithe-looking yet feet-on-the-ground blonde, thirtyish and wearing a dog-collar, swapped a few words with Daddy and introduced her husband, a blacksmith.

'She's applied for the living at Lower Buxcomb,' he remarked.

'A welcome whiff of religious femininity,' I said.

'Yes. Perhaps Anglo-Saxon priestesses are making a come-back?'

'Shall she offer libations to Woden at the full moon?'

'Who *knows* … ' he howled.

'So childish,' I laughed. 'I'm thinking of taking Anglo-Saxon in my final year.'

The last priest at Lower Buxcomb had been defrocked for sleeping with his *au pair*. It sounded as if she had been 'defrocked' too, but so as not to lower the tone, I kept quiet.

Daddy shook his head. 'Biblical Hebrew's tough and the Early Byzantine History … then a second difficult language?'

'Yet I do like them.'

'My room-mate at Cambridge did some Anglo-Saxon … and the verbs were so irregular.'

'But an eighth-century Northumbrian thane would, I suppose, only need about ten of them?'

'Oh well, there's a Noël Coward saying, "Work is more fun than fun."'

'Also to pass this degree, you are allowed to fail one of the nine sections.'

Mummy had of course put Osric in the guest's bedroom.

Daddy and I were the last to go upstairs. I knelt before him and took his hands. 'I so love him. You must be kind to him.'

He held my head in his hands, leant forwards and kissed my forehead. 'We will. I promise.'

I took my large doll Lucy from off the chair by my desk, put her in bed with me and fell asleep.

Osric tried to forestall any trip to Maryport.

'No. I want to meet your family,' I insisted.

The street was dismal, with no colour or signs of life. The terrace-houses were flat-fronted, stood next to the pavement and had those heavy sandstone lintels and door-steps so typical of Cumbria. Curtains were either dowdy or drawn and the doors and window-frames had flaking paint.

I wore a new black woollen coat over a white silk blouse with a mini-jabot at the collar, a pleated MacAlpine tartan skirt and a dark-green cardigan. Osric had said, 'You're mad. We're not visiting a palace.'

As we entered the narrow hallway, Osric's mother and his sister Sharon were having a row and they barely cast a glance at us.

There seemed to be clutter everywhere. Osric said, 'We're trying to win the National Squalor Week award.'

He sat me on a sagging sofa in which the springs seemed to have gone, but I stood up again as he eventually managed to introduce his mother.

'Pleased to meet you,' she said with a brief but half-hearted smile. We sat down and she started playing a game on her laptop.

Sharon entered too with a bun and a cup of tea she had made for herself and lit a cigarette which she dropped on the floor and had to retrieve from under a cupboard. There was a damp musty smell in the room. Everything really needed to go into a skip.

Sharon wore a white plasticky crinoline blouse and a black rubbery mini-skirt with a few chrome-plated D-rings and lengths of chain drooping from its belt. It made Sophie's leather mini-skirt look quite posh by contrast.

Whilst Osric went to make tea, I watched the war game. Japanese soldiers were fighting American ones. When she fired at a G.I., either it missed or it blew out the whole of his torso; never did it just clip an arm.

Tea appeared, but there was no milk.

Sharon rang her boyfriend and as a telephonic spat took off, went upstairs to rant and shout in the confines of her own room.

Mother and Sharon were on the dole, the brother in prison for robbery and the father had disappeared some years ago.

I glimpsed an official letter lying on the floor. Mother had it seemed falsely claimed crisis credit for an allegedly broken cooker.

'Where's Mandy?' I asked.

Osric had said that this sister was quite sweet and that he and she were quite close. 'In rehab.'

'Where?'

'Near Carlisle.'

'Let's go and visit her?'

With a deep breath, he stood up. I followed and we left.

Mother, down-trodden and depressed, was too busy zapping enemy infantry to say farewell.

There was an unpaid electric bill lying on the hall mat. I picked it up. 'We'll pay this.'

Outside he almost wept. He put his head in his hands and said, 'God, I feel so ashamed.'

I took his wrists. 'It doesn't matter,' I insisted.

We drove to Carlisle.

'One day Mandy spent seven hours trying to find a vein. She must have stabbed herself hundreds of times.'

'We'll stop and buy her something ... chocolates and a nice bouquet of flowers ... not very original, but it shows good intent.'

'I don't think it matters.'

'Osric,' I said firmly, 'it *does* matter.'

'Stop telling me what to do!'

I stopped the car.

Sibylle had met Osric briefly and afterwards knitted her brows. 'Couldn't you find someone more ... er ... refined?'

I had replied, 'If you're in love, you don't think like that.'

Sibylle was very attractive, yet also very sober and evaluating; very Germanic.

Yet there were moments when I wondered, but then I sensed God or Jeremiah; 'This is the right path. Stick with it.' Then God would bless me and I knew, without question, that it was the right path.

I burst into tears.

The rehabilitation centre, though built quite recently was already showing signs of neglect and decline.

I had not realised that the flowers and chocolates would be such a huge issue. The staff assume that you are smuggling in drugs. Eventually they allowed them through. The staff themselves looked pretty wooden.

Mandy did seem quite a sweet girl, as Osric had said. The other three inmates we met looked thoroughly nasty. Mandy was quite simple and gullible. She had worked in a bakery and somehow just fallen in with a bad crowd in the evenings, but she was not basically bad. How had she got into this mess? You could weep for her. I hugged her tightly and gave her a kiss before we set off for Newcastle.

'Can't she stay at home?'

'Mum won't let her. Last time she stole her laptop to sell, to pay for a fix.'

Having failed my Phoenician paper and so needing to resit it, I had to get down to some revision.

After a day of such, I had promised to go to Osric's flat in Tynemouth, which I did not do very often.

Outside I met Adrian.

'There's someone else watching your flat now.'

'Someone else?'

'Fat this time, not thin.'

'Is he watching our flat or the downstairs one?'

'It's not possible to tell.'

The lads had played with a Ouija board one night and although not superstitious, it had scared the wits out of them. Not daring to go to bed, they had noticed him from their front window, until well past one o'clock.

'Take a photo, if you have the chance.'

'It's in the evenings ... and he keeps to the shadows.'

This sounded a bit worrying.

'Where are you off to?'

'Tynemouth ... to see my boyfriend.'

Osric's flat was in a somewhat rundown Victorian mansion named Como House.

He had found a new recipe; sausages, salami chunks and lentils with onions, garlic, tinned tomatoes and bay leaves. Despite its simplicity, having simmered for a couple of hours, it was very tasty.

Osric slept on the couch in his main room since the tiny bedroom was littered with bits of a toy railway, ancient Greek soldiers and French Foreign Legionnaires who stood guard on a quaint white wooden fort.

At first I thought he seemed either quiet or just a bit down, but then realised that he looked a little pale or even greenish. When I held him too, he was distinctly feverish.

Whilst I washed up and he made coffee, I noted that he moved unsteadily and seemed mentally inattentive.

'Do you feel unwell?'

He stared at me. 'I've had a headache all day.'

'You don't usually suffer from headaches?'

'No.'

I decided to stay the night and soon after this he vomited up his dinner.

As I made up the couch, he fell onto his knees, became dizzy and then semi-conscious.

I fell onto my knees too and held him. 'It's all right. I've got you.'

Then he started to fit, with slow but jerky convulsions. With some effort I steadied him, lowered him onto the carpet and then rolled him onto his side.

In tears, I restrained him gently until his spasms lessened. I hugged him and watched his breathing. It seemed regular, though it varied in depth. He was delirious for a spell, but as he bordered on the unconscious, I had to call an ambulance.

On day three, on my third visit to the infectious diseases ward in the Royal Victoria Infirmary, they had finally fixed on a diagnosis; Japanese encephalitis.

He was unwell, though not dangerously so.

Perhaps rather foolishly, I climbed onto the bed. We were propped up semi-vertically on the pillows and I was on top of the covers whilst Osric was under them, but even so, I was soon told to get off.

'But it is good for him … to be loved and stroked?'

'Off!'

As I stood up, a sheet of doodled Phoenician words floated onto the floor.

'What's this? Black magic?' asked the sister.

Claude had been to see Osric and said he was sorry, but as a three-man business, he could not afford to keep him on.

'Don't worry. We'll be all right. And Daddy will help if we're really stuck. He says that the strange thing about money, is that although there's never enough, there's always enough to do that which you need to do.'

A spider descended in front of my eyes. I stood up nipped its thread between finger and thumb and – using alternate hands – kept hoisting it up to see if it would exhaust its supply of goo and start climbing back up. Then I spotted the sister in the distance watching me. She of course could not see the spider. I bent over and laughed.

In my resit exam, one unseen translation was an epitaph from Carthage, which I had previously unpicked myself. In the second, King Ithobaal of Tyre's name appeared in an irregular vocative form which by luck I had also come across. This inscription alluded too to his daughter, the Biblical Jezebel.

Osric was less lucid in the evenings. I caressed my poor beloved and told him, that one day we would live in an old country railway station and have five children.

He frowned. His grandfather, on watch in a fox-hole one night in Burma had heard some movement. 'There were two bare wire ends which when touched together rang a buzzer at the main guard-post back in the compound and … ' He lost the thread.

I wiped his face and neck with a cold wet flannel and combed his hair. He re-awoke and quoted Kipling:

'When you're wounded and left on Afghanistan's plains,
And the women come out to cut up what remains,
Just roll on your rifle and blow out your brains
And go to your God like a soldier.'

I cuddled him. 'Never. An angel will rescue you.'
Caught in Thailand, it had an incubation period

of five to fifteen days, seizures were common, there were no specific cures ... just rest, fluids, pain killers and febrifuges. Thirty per cent die and forty per cent of survivors continue to have neurological or cognitive symptoms.

He was on the mend – he was eating again and shaving himself – so on a whim, on my next visit, I took in a little bottle of perfume. It was called 'Boadicea' and was made from petals of *Rose de Mai*. It was a very expensive English brand and had been a present from Oberon Films for my winning the prize *The Garland of Wild Parsley*.

It was afternoon and the sun shone in rhomboids through the tall windows of the spacious Nightingale ward and for twenty minutes I walked up and down with Osric.

All seemed quiet. Many patients were asleep and the two nurses at the far end were both fixed on their computer screens.

Osric sat down on the chair beside his bed and with an impish smile, I knelt down, removed his thick socks and put his bare feet on a towel. I then unscrewed the pear-shaped bottle and rubbed the perfume all over his feet.

No one would have known – other than the guy watching from the next bed – except that an exquisite fragrance drifted down the length of the ward.

Osric grinned.

I giggled.

The senior sister appeared. 'What on earth are you doing?'

'Wiping his feet.'

She walked off and no more was said.

I left half an hour later after giving him my usual kiss.

As I left, a patient at the farthest end of the ward shouted down to the nurses that the guy next to him was blue and not breathing.

Walking down the stairs I was nearly knocked over by four young housemen with bleeps squawking as they raced past me. I guessed they were junior doctors, who once would have been identifiable by white coats, but now wore trainers and T-shirts. Apart from their bleeps, they were no different to many of the visitors.

Before reaching Otterburn Terrace, I stopped and bought a large pizza.

Sophie bade me sit beside her.

'Yes, Miss Muffet?'

She prodded a yellow coloured card. 'In Classical Greek, "girl" is "kore". 'Homer uses the earlier Ionic "kourwa".'

'And the blue card?'

'The Doric, "kora".'

'Your curds and whey are going cold, dearest.'

'From this, the archaic form "korwa", was extrapolated … and in Arcadian – the oldest dialect we know – that is what it is.'

'So, concurrence? Bravo,' I munched.

'It's so shadowy and remote,' she enthused softly, now also through a mouthful of crust with Hawaiian topping, 'a time so misty and obscure … We can scarcely penetrate their primitive minds.'

The door-bell rang. I went down and let in Kiyoshi.

He no longer bowed or showed deference. The intimidating effect which western women exert on Oriental men had worn off.

Sophie ignored him. 'So the classical Athenian loses the digamma – the "w" – and changes the final alpha to an eta, thus giving "kore".'

Kiyoshi glowered and snatched unbidden, a slice of pizza, but he did not scare Miss Muffet.

Some hasty impulse had swept her into this puerile liaison, egged on probably by his helping her with her studies.

'Move these cards, so I can sit down.'

'No.'

There was an ominous silence.

'So, it amuses you to be sexually titillating and then not let anything happen?'

I stared at him.

'And when I'm not here, laugh?'

'You horrible ogre!' I rasped.

'Don't you interfere.'

'I shall if you insult her.'

He fumed. 'Why can you girls advance or withhold yourselves at will; tease without fear of retaliation? We men are just playthings to be mocked and milked … It shouldn't be like this!'

Sophie stood up and told him to go.

This tousled, pink-eyed, yellow-skinned, humourless mutt hesitated, then grabbed her upper arm.

I jumped up, but before I could assist, she had bent his right arm up behind his back and he was doubled over in agony.

After half a minute, she let go and pointed to the stairs. 'Out.'

I added my eye-ball fire to hers and looking blacker than thunder, he left.

She shouted after him, '*Cau'r drws,*' then grinned. This apparently is Welsh for 'Close the door.'

At around ten, we heard some shouting outside but could see nothing. Then came the flashing blue light of a police car.

Rob, heading for the corner shop, had seen the fat guy loitering suspiciously and then bumped into a young policewoman and told her. She then spotted the loiterer hiding in a front garden and tried to question him, but he had shoved her suddenly and forcefully into some overgrown bushes and run off with a lumbering gait. It took the girl a minute to extricate herself and by the time she tried to chase after him, she could not see where he had gone. She radioed a description so that any patrol vehicle in the area could keep a lookout and when Rob reappeared with his shopping, took his details, gave him a crime number and told him to call if he saw this lout again.

Next day, Sophie intended to visit her cousin in Manchester, so I dropped her off at the station before visiting my fiancé again.

As I walked onto the ward the junior sister saw me and beckoned me into the little kitchen at the end of the ward where the breakfasts and teas were prepared.

'Are you Mary Fleet?'

'Yes.'

'I'm sorry, but we're not to allow you onto the ward.'

'What?'

'We've been told that you might be a danger to the patients … and to us.'

'By whom?'

'A social worker. He even said that we should cover our name badges if you appeared and be ready to call the police.'

I was just speechless.

'But you don't look dangerous.'

I was actually quite nicely dressed. 'Can I see these instructions?'

'Well … I think they're only verbal.'

'But … doesn't something like that have to be official?'

'I suppose so … but social workers often seem reluctant to write things down.'

'So … whispers in back corridors?'

'I know. Look I've no objection. I'll just say I didn't see you.'

I managed to thank her. She was young, serious and decent. You could see that quite plainly.

I walked up and down with Osric again, before we had tea and cherry tarts in the day-room. I did not mention the social worker threat as I had no wish to disturb him. I was though inwardly quite shaken.

The page of Phoenician lettering had acquired some columns of figures. 'Three of us played sergeant-major yesterday.'

'They sometimes play that in our church hall … with a snowball prize.'

'They plan to discharge me on Saturday.'

'Excellent.' I cuddled him.

Next morning, as I vacuum-cleaned the flat, the door-bell rang.

It was the fat guy called David from the English literature students' party.

'What do you want?'

He showed me his social worker's identity fob, which I inspected. 'Can I come in?'

'I repeat, what do you want?'

'It's official … and it's rather confidential. I think it would be better if we spoke in private.'

Reluctantly I led the way up the stairs. I had not yet linked him with yesterday's ward ban.

'Well?'

'We've had some very disturbing reports about your behaviour in the Royal Victoria Infirmary and we think it would be advisable for you to see a psychiatrist.'

'Are you crazy?'

'Mary, we understand that you are having an emotionally difficult time,' he said with lard-like smirking features.

I knew that he was lusting after me. 'Well you can just get out!'

'Mary, you are not being sensible. Can we just sit down and talk?'

'No!'

'You could end up in trouble … or face restrictions if you're uncooperative.'

'And what does that mean?'

'Mary we're here to help you … to support you.'

'Not threaten me? Put something bad on my CRB if I don't cringe and let you interfere in my life?'

Suddenly I realised that he was behind the hospital ban. 'I want you to get out … now! I suppose you usually deal with the impaired or confused, who are unable to complain coherently?'

He smiled unpleasantly. Not only was he grossly fat and with four chins, but he looked repugnant.

He showed no signs of leaving and even perhaps moved a little towards me, such that I backed away.

Suddenly I glimpsed Adrian crossing the street. I threw up the window and shouted – almost screamed – 'Adrian, come and help me!'

Fatso was blocking the way to the stairwell so I could not go to open the door. I thought my keys were in my skirt pocket, but when I padded it they were not. Adrian stood on the path looking up.

I was in tears. 'Just get in! I need help!'

He gave a grim nod, reversed a few paces, then charged the door like a bull.

I heard the door-frame splinter and the door thump back against the wall.

I collapsed on the sofa in tears. Fatso disappeared and Adrian, after holding my hands and comforting me, called the police and then made tea.

'I bet that's the guy who Rob saw.'

An hour later Adrian and I had made our statements to two constables and a carpenter had set about mending the door-frame.

'If these no-good bastards had less shifty and labyrinthine assignments, they might actually become men. Look at Guy Gibson, a squadron leader at twenty-four?'

I nodded.

Around tea-time a sergeant and a female constable appeared.

They had discussed the matter with the head of the relevant social services outfit, who said that sadly those with mental health issues often turned on those trying to help them. Such misrepresentations were not unusual. Those in need of help are often resistant or misunderstand what is being offered and indeed sometimes lie or hallucinate in order to cover their own defects. 'We are assured that David Fraser is held in the highest esteem by his professional colleagues, has been a registered social worker for five years ... and that the department operates within very strict guidelines and to the highest ethical standards.'

'Have you inspected their file ... to see the order that he gave to the ward staff at the hospital?'

'Their files are confidential. We are not permitted access to them. Only a high court judge can order that.'

I managed a thin sardonic smile. 'Giving them time to doctor anything which might prove awkward?'

They left.

No outsider will ever be able to prove anything against this bunch. They will portray you as the one who is deranged. And even if Fraser's colleagues suspected the truth, they would cover for him and stick together. They are the judge and jury of their own actions. 'Concern' is the code-word they use for control, for coercion, for imposing their 'neutral' values. If you refuse their 'help' then clearly there is something wrong with you and you need to be put on various watch lists. A state within a state. The stealthy dictators of modern Britain.

As I slept, a spirit told me not to be bitter. My avenger would be God, through some recondite act.

Next day a Special Delivery letter appeared. I was apparently showing classical symptoms of schizophrenia – a morbid emotional detachment and thought discrepancy patterns – and was strongly advised to accept their offer of a fast-track appointment with their psychiatric support team worker.

If sanity is the consensus of the majority, the local authority's social idealists – like the troops of an occupying force's fortress – are without that majority.

We all need something greater than ourselves, whether God or loyalty or love. It seemed that I had all three and they hated me for it.

To defuse my rage, I wrote a reply:

'Dear Jill Vickerton,

Mr Fraser says he wants my vulva instead of his Volvo.

He uses Ariel washing powder. Ariel was an angel and that is why he is so extra white.

Are men in white coats on their way to arrest me and to turn me into a robot?

Scorpions store their poison in an impermeable sac, but if one is tickled on its back with a straw, it will bring over its sting and kill itself. So Jill, beware no one tickles your back … '

I tore it into tiny pieces.

Adrian came round and read my Special Delivery letter. 'You are one of the most sound-minded people I know.'

'You need to be on your guard too, Adrian. They might strike first ... to discredit you?'

'Attack is the best form of defence ... and keeping their ivory tower safe is definitely their top task.'

That evening Sophie returned and I told her my story.

As well as coffee, she poured herself a brandy and said nothing for a time. I had more or less given up on her saying anything at all, when she said, 'I've heard of social workers adjusting their "case" histories – to forestall criticism – but nothing at this level. "Despicable" isn't strong enough.'

That seemed to be it until the next afternoon, when she knocked, came into my room and sat down. 'I've discovered two things about David Fraser.'

'Oh?'

'One, where he lives and two, that tonight he's going to a "Whodunnit" dinner, near Rothbury.'

'How did you discover that?'

She knelt down and picked up my Bible. 'Kneel down.'

I did so, but was puzzled.

'You swear to me that what I am going to tell you, you will *never* betray to anyone.'

I was mystified but put my hand on the Bible, swore by the Trinity and crossed myself.

She leant forwards, held me and whispered in my ear.

I straightened up and blinked. I had vaguely wondered. When in London and she had supposedly gone to the British Museum, she had not afterwards remarked on a single exhibit.

All this fitted. Sophie could be disarmingly honest, yet at other times quite evasive.

And so that evening at ten o'clock, in pouring rain, we arrived in Fenham at a row of gloomy nondescript terrace-houses.

Wearing dark coats, gloves and scarves wound round the lower halves of our faces, we traversed the narrow front garden. No lights were on and no one answered the bell.

'It's a cylinder lock, but an older type.' Choosing carefully from her bunch of keys in the dim rays from a nearby street-light, the second one she tried did the trick and we were in.

I was terrified but Sophie seemed pretty much at ease. We stood still for a minute and listened.

We put some lights on and poked about in the kitchen and the main room. 'Nothing here,' she said.

Upstairs it was the same story for the front bedroom and the bathroom, but when we opened the door to the smaller bedroom – which unusually opened outwards – we were confronted with a second solid-looking door which had a large brass padlock on it.

My knees were practically knocking.

On her huge key-ring were some thin metal probes and one of these she poked into this padlock. Within say forty seconds it popped open.

I must have looked goggle-eyed.

She whispered, 'The first three or four hundred are tricky. After that it's usually fairly easy.'

The room was about ten foot square. There were two large pictures of myself taken at the awards ceremony on the wall and three of Sibylle, taken at odd angles and so presumably from under cover. There was an old iron bedstead – probably Victorian – and on it a cardboard box full of leather belts, frilly items of female underwear and handcuffs. I took a dozen pictures. On the desk, beside the computer, were various letters. We slipped into our shopping bag a bank statement, an invoice for tonight's 'Escape from Colditz' party and two computer memory sticks, before going through the drawers.

We took a folder of what might have been copies of poison-pen letters and another of pictures of women, some with obscene additions drawn on them in crayon.

Framed on the wall were his 'A' level certificates; an E in economics and a D in politics. He had attended Marlborough School and had written an imprecation across their shield.

He was probably one of those council-house boys who had been funded by a trades union scholarship, but had not fitted in with public school life and so ended up hating the school, the establishment and everything else to do with our country. No team spirit; no pride in collaborative achievement.

With a lipstick, Sophie drew a huge question-mark on the wall.

Otherwise we left everything as it had been, replacing the padlock and switching off the lights.

We walked the half-mile back to my car, by which time my heart rate had perhaps dropped below the hundred and thirty mark.

'Probably wisest to do nothing more for a bit. Just knowing someone's been there will frighten him.'

Quite an understatement, I thought.

Later in bed, I cuddled Titus. I whispered to him, 'That's the most nerve-wracking thing I've ever done.'

CHAPTER SEVENTEEN

Sophie set off for Harlech.

'Give a ring, if you want to come and stay. Mum and Dad have gone to Cyprus for a couple of weeks.'

Adrian – still marked with shock – came round before setting off for his summer break.

'The cover-up is really worse than the original crime.'

'The crime at its point of interception?' I took his arms. 'I cannot properly thank you.'

'Well ... just lucky I was there.' He thought a little. 'If our only recourse is also to play dirty, suppose we addressed an envelope to Fraser at his office, with some dosh in it, an anonymous note thanking him for fixing up our mother in a care home and some white powder stuck to the outside, such that toxicologists or the bomb-squad would be called in to open it?'

I smiled. 'No, let's not do anything like that. Something might occur to turn the tables?'

'I doubt it. Anyway, just a random thought. Besides, I don't have five hundred quid to spare.'

'No.'

Again he grew serious. 'Mary, my gut feeling is that lust was not his principal motivation.'

'Oh?'

'My guess is that he hates you for your integrity or your decency and so wants to degrade you.'

I shrugged. 'We shall never know. With Iago, Shakespeare does not explain his motive. He just *is* nasty?'

We wished one another well and he set off for his parents' home in Winchester.

I rang Osric. 'Is all well my love? Me? Of course. Especially on hearing your voice.'

'Did you meet Arlene?'

'Arlene?'

'The junior sister. She's given me a print-out.' He stopped.

'Go on.'

'It's from a local authority lawyer to the hospital's chief executive, regarding a ban on your visiting here?'

'Carry on.'

'It says that at no time was such an instruction given by any of their staff and that so far as they are concerned, you are free to visit.'

'Osric, just keep it safe. I'll explain when we're together.'

'Arlene asked that we do not give her as its source.'

'Are you still eating well?'

'Yes. Toad-in-the-hole is just being served up.'

'Splendid.' We exchanged hushed farewells.

I eyed my Swedish engagement ring and kissed it.

Alone, I saw my enemies bent over their gaming-board. 'Second Panzer Division to encircle Otterburn Terrace.'

Could they say I 'lacked capacity' and ask a judge to section me? And who would he believe?

I bundled some stuff into the car – all important documents, four text-books and some clothes – before driving out to Tynemouth. I stopped at a supermarket to buy a cheap pay-as-you-go mobile phone and turned off my usual one. I rang Daddy, Osric and Sophie to give them this clandestine new number.

I parked near the seafront, which was some distance from Osric's flat, then lugged my stuff – though buffeted by a strong wind – to Como House where I let myself in to his first-floor pad.

I chewed over various *ruses de guerre*. A play of insanity might excuse strange acts, but also provide grounds for their locking me up. As with writing essays, such plans require 'reverse extrapolation'. You write paragraph one only when you see the intended end-point.

I knelt down with Osric's toys. The toy train was pre-war. The engine was attached to three wagons, the van tin-printed with 'Colman's Mustard'. On the tin platform stood flour sacks, lamps, enamelled adverts for Bovril and Hudson's Soap, lead passengers and beside it, a tall semaphore signal. I pushed the train round on the tracks and then into a siding.

Early toy trains were play-things rather than models. Scale and accuracy were sacrificed for character or a distinctive stamp.

On the fort, some of the Foreign Legionnaires leant on the battlements, aiming their rifles. A fat Fraser-like passenger from the station, I placed before the fort, then commanded the legionnaires; '*Aux armes! Ouvrons le feu! Pan, pan, pan.*' The fat man fell over.

I had decided to take Biblical Hebrew instead of Arabic, since I would not now be becoming a travel rep in Morocco. Clutching a calligraphy pen, I settled down to practise the alphabet and the pointing, which is all the dots and dashes which were added later to indicate vowels, breaks and so forth. I was soon very absorbed; a good and calming distraction.

At nine o'clock, I stretched and looked out of the French windows. Except for the wind, all was quiet. I closed the curtains and put a pizza in the oven.

The entrance buzzer buzzed. I froze. It buzzed again. My heart pounded.

After a time knuckles rapped on the door. They had somehow entered and come up the stairs. I ran to the window and peeped between the curtains. A taxi stood there.

Again a rap on the door. So persistent. Would they kick it in? I decided I had to open it.

Two men stood there, smiling.

One was a neighbour. 'I hope you don't mind? I let him in. I saw your lights were on.'

'Oh, er ... thank you.'

'Mary Fleet?' The taxi driver handed me a large envelope.

Struggling to slow my breathing down and look serene, I thanked him too and closed the door.

I fumbled to open the envelope and extracted the *Tyneside Gazette* as if it might be a bomb.

On its front, in red crayon, it read, 'See page six. Rob.'

A red ring circled an article about a 'Whodunnit' dinner at a country house near Rothbury, a popular venue for weddings and similar events.

The pizza was overdone or 'crisp' as you might say.

The headline read: 'Dinner Extravaganza ends in disarray.'

One devotee, who had an escort agency girl with him to supply some glamour, had developed a tightness in his chest. The summoned ambulance became stuck in boggy grass as it turned and then a fire engine, trying to pull it out, slipped sideways towards the edge of a duck pond where its wheels simply spun. Eventually a heavy recovery vehicle with a winch had hauled both back onto the metalled driveway.

This pantomime had lasted until three in the morning.

A spokeswoman for the Newcastle General Hospital described David Fraser's condition as 'stable'.

I recited Psalm forty-nine: 'Be not afraid in evil times, when beset by treacherous foes. Like sheep they are headed to Sheol.' Jeremiah knew his foes were headed for captivity. I recited a second psalm, number forty-six: 'Be still and know that I am God.'

In bed – that is on Osric's couch – I cuddled his pillow.

At five in the morning, I awoke with a vague sense of panic.

I drank tea, loaded up my little Fiat Panda and by six had set off. I broke my journey to fill up with petrol and buy two rolls of electrical tape from an ironmonger's; one white and one yellow. From a branch of my bank, I took out fifteen hundred pounds so as to avoid using my bank card again for a while.

In a secluded lay-by, I stuck squares of the white and yellow tape onto my car's number plates, converting one E into an L and the second into an F. I suppose this does quite rank with James Bond, but one has to start somewhere.

It rained heavily for most of the way.

To such men as Fraser, life's beauty and its terrors do not speak of heaven and hell. The world's unforgiving nature – you would think – would persuade even thistledown to seek a comelier form to its brief existence.

One client of Uncle Basil's, in challenging the approval of a fraudulent planning application, had in seeking some middle ground owned up to two trivial oversights. These though were then simply turned against him. He had suggested too dropping his complaint if they apologised, but Uncle Basil had said, 'They won't buy it. They won't trust you. The devious assume that everyone is devious.'

He had also hinted that chief constables have something known as 'Drawer 13', where they hide crimes which are *not* to be investigated.

At one o'clock, stiff and weary, I reached Harlech.

The bungalow – a pre-fab constructed of concrete panels bolted together and painted cream and with an asbestos or tin roof painted green – looked modest though well-tended. In front lay a ragged strip of lawn, a neat fence of green palings on a rough stone retaining wall and a bed of limp cornflowers. It stood at the bottom of the hill, below the castle and near to the railway station and was backed by bushes and a rocky slope.

A cat stared at me and meowed. Sophie came out and gave an unsurprised smile.

'There are very few pre-fabs left,' she said. 'They were put up just after the war, not very elegant but quite solid and easy to assemble I'm told.'

In the kitchen, over tea and toast, she absorbed my 'trailless escape' with mild scepticism.

'If you do seem to have disappeared though, they'll have to start a search ... to show their "concern". They are after all peddling the line that you're unbalanced.'

We hid my car behind a Mrs Williams' cottage and removed its number plates. 'She's in hospital,' said Sophie, 'but she won't mind.'

Whilst she read the *Tyneside Gazette* report from Rothbury, I picked up her giant bunch of keys which lay on the matt-black unlit iron stove with its lagged chimney pipe going up through the roof. I looked at the flat metal strips, one of which had opened Fraser's padlock.

Sophie pointed. 'That's a rake, that's a half-moon and that's a half-diamond.'

'How do they work?'

'They explore the wider tolerances. It's said that if all a lock's components were perfectly made, you couldn't pick it.'

We wrote out flash cards using coloured crayons – we both still had a childish streak – mine Biblical Hebrew and Sophie's classical Greek, to test one other. During my school days, Emily and I had done the same with our Latin and French. In both Greek and Hebrew the letters are not joined up.

Next morning we went to a care home near Porthmadog. A great-aunt had died recently and Sophie was to collect her belongings.

The manager in a crumpled brown suit, with a pony-tail and a seedy-looking face, wrung his hands. 'Such a sad occasion.'

I actually laughed.

We took away two cartons of Aunt Cerys's possessions which turned out to be all rubbish. 'What's this?' I asked. 'Her wedding ring?'

Sophie inspected it. 'It's just gilded plastic ... out of a Christmas cracker probably. They've nicked the real one.'

Rob forwarded a 'missing persons' notice to Sophie's phone. It had been posted across the northern press.

The photo of my upper-body – taken at the Cinematic Awards ceremony – had been deftly underexposed, a technique used by totalitarian regimes when depicting an 'enemy of the state'. I appeared sinister and hollow-eyed. The wild parsley garland too, intimated Hamlet's Ophelia going mad and about to drown herself.

'Mary Fleet, nineteen and assessed as being seriously mentally ill has gone missing. Social Services are concerned for her safety and wish to contact her urgently and give her support. We ask anyone with information to contact the police or social services.'

'We're sages, amateur polymaths ... and we're going to win.'

We saw a police car parked near the pre-fab, so we drove on by and out to the dunes where we paddled in the sea.

Up in the town, we went into a grocer's shop. The bell pinged, I tripped on a sack of green beans, we bought bars of local unwrapped soap and I eyed the old scales with their set of brass weights and a brass scoop-shaped pan on one side.

'A quarter of liquorice toffees, please.'

The next day, Sophie took her mother's car in for its M.O.T. whilst I did the household chores.

A strong wind blew and I had not heard the car pull up. As I went out to the dust-bin, a rather up-herself tweed-clad woman came towards me.

She smiled stiffly. 'Good morning. I'm seeking a Miss Sophie Hughes?' She thrust an I.D. badge towards my face.

'Yes? Sophie Igraine Hughes?' I said in a deliberately level tone, such that it might be construed as a statement or as a question.

'We've been asked to ask you if you know of the whereabouts of a Mary Fleet?'

'If I do know, am I obliged to tell?'

'She is in urgent need of help, so it would be inhumane, even cruel, to refuse.'

'One of your colleagues in the north tried to ravish her ... and despite evidence of this, his bosses refuse to act.'

She took a slow deep breath. 'Do you really believe that?'

'It was witnessed by her neighbour.'

After an equine-like shuddery snort, she said, 'Well, if I cannot persuade you to help, then on your conscience be it.' She turned on her heel and walked briskly off.

How lucky I was to have been paired with Sophie by the University's accommodation office.

From the radio of a workman next door came a line from a Beatles' song; 'When I think about you I can say, I'm never, never, never blue.' I needed to love Osric as that bee humming drowsily amid the celandine needed nectar. Yet the rancid honey of that visit to Maryport? I recalled a couplet by Catullus:

'I love and I hate. You inquire, "Why so?"
Lo cloven my fate, 'twixt desire and woe.'

Speaking by telephone, Osric mentioned a railway station he had seen for sale in Northumberland. 'It's a total ruin … but we couldn't buy it anyway.'

I did not answer.

'Oh and I've sent two pictures to Sophie. Did you ever meet Nurse Cain?'

'No.'

'From Wallsend? She asked with a wry grin if I were looking forward to being discharged, so that I could see you again?'

'Oh?'

'We were stood at the nurses' station. She brought up my page on the Nursing Kardex and indicated the "Additional instructions" box. I asked to take a photo of it. She shrugged, let me and then stretched it to expand the critical bit for a second shot.

The Kardex is updated each shift, but no one had thought to erase this.

Later, when she asked if I would delete the photos, I promised that if we showed them to anyone, we would hide her name and log-in details.'

The box read: 'As instructed by the social worker Mr David Fraser, a Miss Mary Fleet is not to be allowed onto the ward due to a history of violence and sending death threats. Staff are to cover their name badges, be watchful that she does not follow them home and to call security if she becomes agitated.'

In cases of Japanese encephalitis which survive, some have a residual tendency to fits and in others some loss of intellect persists. Osric though sounded well enough.

Sophie's parents returned. She said I could stay as my sleeping-bag on top of Megan's bed was no impediment, but I thought it time to leave.

Branwen and Taffy were quite knock-about and cheerful, indeed almost boisterous. I said to Sophie how infectious was their vitality.

'Yes,' she conceded without enthusiasm. 'In small doses. Very small.'

I had driven barely ten miles, when it struck me that Uncle Basil might be able to advise me. I rang him from a lay-by and it was an unexpectedly friendly and easy exchange.

They had a little holiday cottage at Ravenglass and were currently there.

'Come and see us, Mary. I'm decorating and would love a break.'

'I can wield a paint brush too, if you wish?'

'I said to Marlene that marriage is one long roll of wallpaper, to which she retorted that it is one huge bowl of washing-up.'

I spent the night at a guest house in Millom.

Ravenglass, where three rivers – the Esk, the Irt and the Mite – meet in a common estuary, had been a Roman port. Flakes of their red-orange tiles are still to be seen in the shallows among the pebbles.

Breakfast in their tiny back garden, consisted of

boiled eggs in blue and gold egg-cups, heather honey from Fortnum's, thickly sliced bread, herb butter and filter coffee.

Beyond the dry-stone wall and a row of prickly bushes lay a meadow with sheep grazing and the sun coming up over the hills.

I sat there in a blue T-shirt, dark-blue shorts and black rubber sandals and related my sorry tale.

My uncle jotted down a chronological synopsis, then despatched an email to the Head of Social Services, outlining my ban from visiting the hospital – issued on their instructions and based on defamatory and untrue allegations – and asking for an explanation and an apology.

'We'll keep the Nursing Kardex photos in abeyance and see if they dig themselves into a hole.'

'From your name, they will know that we're related?'

'Lawyers are not barred from acting for family members and if I'm representing my niece, they will know that I'm likely to be more thorough.'

I spent the entire morning with a wire brush, a coarse file and some emery-cloth cleaning the wrought-iron front gate and its posts and then painting them with an anti-rust black paint.

After lunch, a reply stated that Mr Fraser's managers had given assurances that no instruction banning my visits had at any time been given to the nursing staff in the Royal Victoria Infirmary and if we wished to take it further, we should contact the hospital directly.

Uncle Basil then sent them the Nursing Kardex shots and in effect said, 'Your witness.'

The reply to this was that they were not prepared to investigate any assertion based on illicitly leaked material and that no further correspondence would be entered into.

Basil and Marlene enjoyed a game of cards, so over coffee and chocolates we played two rounds, each of three hands, of Black Maria, during which he said, 'To sue for libel would be civil, very expensive, they would engage top barristers and if all their people flatly deny it, the outcome is far from sure.'

'So perjury?'

'Oh, that wouldn't worry them at all.'

I left in the early evening; a very amicable and satisfying day.

CHAPTER EIGHTEEN

The Northumberland Central Railway should have run from Scotsgap up to the Scottish border, but financial difficulties meant that – in spite of its impressive title – it ended up as an impoverished rural branch line which terminated at Rothbury.

It drizzled and cloud hung over the shallow valley as we stood on the narrow stone bridge and looked down at the weed-covered track-bed and the tiny desolate station.

The 'For Sale' sign looked mouldy and dismal.

We wandered down the muddy and overgrown footpath, between chest-high rosebay and briars and then poked about in its four derelict rooms. The walls were solid, made of cut ashlars of local stone, but everything else had either vanished or rotted. It came with a ten-acre bramble-filled pasture.

We said nothing as we drifted in and around it, as if waiting for some divine revelation.

Throaty growls heralded a tractor coming down the lane. It drew up and the farmer, who turned out to be the owner, jumped down.

'Osric and Mary.'

'Jim Cowley, Haycomb Farm. Time for hay-making in that field yonder ... Blue Rigg meadow ... but we need a drier spell, with some wind and sun first.'

'When was the station last used?'

'The line closed to passengers in fifty-two and for goods in sixty-three, but the old gate-keeper from

Brinkburn lived here until seventy-five and since then it's just gone to rack and ruin.'

We nodded thoughtfully.

'It had mains electricity,' he pointed to the poles carrying an overhead cable, 'but no mains water or sewerage. On that stretch of line,' he waved a hand, 'I took down the old fences and ploughed it over so its just part of that field again ... as it was I suppose before eighteen-seventy.'

'The "meadow" with it is full of brambles?'

'Well, I hired a tractor once for another field like that. It had a huge propeller on the front, protected with a hood and you just drove it through them and it destroyed them. I worried at first that there might be a huge boulder in a clump that would wreck it ... but there never was.'

We could do little more than nod. 'I'm trying to imagine what it might look like, if we could restore it.'

Mr Cowley rubbed his chin. 'I suppose that depends on how much money you have?'

We nodded solemnly, since we had no available money.

'When I bought it back from British Rail, it cost two thousand pounds. The track had been taken up and that high-grade steel would have been worth more than the land.'

'The auction's in two weeks at *The White Knight*?'

'It is. I've had in on the market for eight months, but no interest ... so it has to be. My granddaughter's brain damaged ... and my daughter needs the money.'

I thought, 'Real flesh and blood, so unlike those poor lost yet smug town-hall apparitions.'

We thanked him and drove off to Morpeth. We were once again using my car.

In the cafeteria of the little department store there, we bought soup and bread rolls.

A girl stopped abruptly and said, 'Hullo Osric.'

It was Staff Nurse Cain.

Osric said, 'Hullo Sylvia.' He assured her once more that we would keep her identity a secret. She sat down briefly.

'Did you know that that David Fraser had a heart attack?'

'We did. At that "Whodunnit" party? Someone showed us a newspaper article.'

'But do you know how it happened?'

'No.'

'Well Fraser, on his fifth serving of chicken, choked on a bone. As he gargled and waved for help and went purple, everyone thought it was an act linked to the detective game. Some even clapped and laughed ... until eventually they realised, thumped his back and cleared his throat. He seemed all right, they said, for twenty minutes ... but then developed the crushing pain in his chest.'

'What an amazing tale?' I said, smiling.

'But there's more to it than that.'

'Oh? Would you like a coffee?'

'No thanks. I'm meeting my brother in a few minutes.'

'Sorry, go on.'

'Well two days ago, he was discharged home. They said his heart rhythm had stabilised and so on, but no sooner did he arrive home than he had another heart attack.'

'Fraser declined to be interviewed, citing ill health. The police girl and I had only seen him in the dark and later identified him from photographs; so not an identity parade. His "attack" on you was dismissed as "unproven" and lastly it was considered "not in the public interest" to undermine confidence in the social services. Summary; the chain of evidence lacks coherence and is therefore unsound.'

I had never really been bitter. My life had been spent, after all, mostly among the upright and fair-minded, yet I was starting to despise these public servants who seemed invariably to shield one another.

An Anglo-Saxon prose piece about a 'witenagemot' – where the chiefs sat on a bench to hear the more serious legal cases – showed a very different spirit.

These wights sought the stability of society and handed out severe penalties to anyone threatening it. Anyone suspected of lies, cop-outs or double-talk, they would come down on heavily.

The door-bell rang.

A police officer stood there of some seniority. He wore no collar number but instead had silver crowns on his epaulettes with red inlays and a silver whistle chain running to the left breast pocket of his jacket.

'Miss Mary Fleet?'

'Yes. Inspector …?'

'Superintendent Lightfoot.'

I led the way upstairs and we sat down.

He started with a few basic questions, as he sought to establish whether I was sensible or screw-ball. I thought his quite shrewd.

'So, he's back in hospital?'

'Yes. On the coronary care unit.'

We thanked her and wished her well, as she patted Osric on the back and took her leave.

One of Sennacherib's cohorts – gleaming in purple and gold – had been smitten by the angel of the Lord.

We were wholly unsure about the dilapidated railway station. The spot had a profound, almost mystical effect and was not too isolated, there being two villages nearby. The work required though was beyond our reserves or ability. 'A mammoth task.'

'Not a mammoth tusk?'

My beloved looked to be on the up and there had been no further epileptic or febrile episodes.

That night we were together again in Otterburn Terrace, in my bed which had sufficient width and a proper mattress and springs. I was on a period, but we pressed ourselves tightly together, such that I could feel his penis against me. He was asleep, but suddenly I felt his sticky ejaculate through my night-dress. I smiled and stoked him. A second if less earthly joy was – as the stoical, diligent and oppressed Jeremiah had also known – that sense that 'The Lord is with me as with a dread warrior.' Soon *they* would fear *me*.

Claude took Osric on again for three days a week and I began to tackle Anglo-Saxon. I needed to finish my degree, if only to make job-finding easier – as a librarian or whatever – afterwards.

A letter from Social Services said that I should return any material I had, which had come from Fraser's house so that it could be restored to its owner.

Sophie eyed it. 'You see that this is a trap? To do that would show that either you are the thief or that you have received stolen goods.'

'They say I have to reply within fourteen days.' I handed her the Manila envelope.

'Of course you don't. It's only a letter. It's not something serious like a parking fine. And make sure you hide all that stuff safely at your parents ... under some floorboards in the attic for instance.'

At Alnmouth, one sunny bright day, Osric and I paddled in the sea and held hands. It seemed perfect ... unlike Thailand.

'Perhaps Farmer Cowley has now mown his grass for silage?'

Yet there were frictions under the surface. As we grow up and change, skirmishes and adjustments are necessary, though at night we forgot them and floated away into some distant Milky Way, one where dusty comets slid passively by and the universe seemed starry and balmy; glinting, harmless and eternal.

I spoke to Daddy about the station for which there was of course no possibility of a mortgage. He had some bank shares he was willing to sell which would give us about fifteen thousand pounds.

The auction was attended by a few curious locals and ourselves.

The reserve was £15,000. We chose to roll the dice and bid up to £18,000, but as it happened, were the only bidders.

In a short medieval comedy, *Elinor of Cleves*, I played Lady Clare de Baddesey; one-scene and four spoken

lines. I wore a mustardy-yellow robe, a w wimple and a wooden pectoral cross. 'You there for ornamentation,' explained the prodt by being shy and endearing ... but graduall more puckish and sceptical.'

This earned just seven hundred and twen after deducting Terry's cut, but money – th previously my main emphasis – did now play just is a part of modern life. We are no long Saxon serfs, where silver pennies would practical use.

Two days later a repair bill came for the Pan together with four new tyres and a complete set-up came to seven hundred and twenty p there a proverb about the world consisting of

Then Chloë rang. A ladies' fashion house ne girls to model for their up-market on-line catalo mother was the assistant director. 'You're a size

'Yes.'

'And I'm a ten, so that makes the pairing Mar they want. Two strenuous days for two thousand

'Oh Chloë, thank you so much.'

'Now Mary, you know that nothing is ev goodness. There's something else?'

'Oh?'

'I'll tell you over our next pasta dish.'

Rob came round. 'The police, recognising Fras one who shoved their young female colleague bushes, charged him with "assaulting a police but the Prosecution Service have rejected it as "u

'Why?'

'We are investigating a break-in to the home of the social worker, David Fraser and your name has been put forward as a suspect.'

I took a deep breath. 'One, I do not know where he lives and two, I would not know how to break into a house ... nor have the courage.'

He gave a slow nod. 'You could have asked a professional to do it for you?'

I pretended to think for a few seconds. 'Even if that crossed my mind, I would not know how to find such a person.'

Another thoughtful nod, then a faint smile. 'Have you any suggestions as to who might be behind it?'

'Well, if he goes round spreading wicked and scurrilous stories, then any of his targets?'

'Hmm.'

'Given his criminal and psychopathic tendencies, you do not think that he might have done it himself?'

He smiled a little more warmly. 'Those who do such usually smash up pictures, urinate on the carpet ... that sort of thing, which a straight burglar would not.'

I shook my head slightly.

He stood up, wished me well and I showed him out.

I perched Titus on my knees. 'Do you remember Guy Fawkes, rolling barrels of gunpowder under the citadel?'

He nodded.

'These town-hall crooks by their deceits are betraying the fragile civilisation handed down to us.' I kissed him. 'Shall I be a pagan priestess and cast a slow-burning curse on this marriage of demons?'

Using one of the library's computers, I researched the

names of nine senior town-hall officials, five councillors and two local M.P.s, printed off address labels and stuck them onto stiffened A4 envelopes. I chose eight of the shots I had taken in Fenham, printed each one sixteen times – whilst wearing gloves and on new unopened stationery – then fed them through the printer again to add the caption, 'David Fraser's padlocked second bedroom.' I drove out to Shiremoor to post them.

The fashion shoot took place in a hotel in Harrogate.

Chloë did the lingerie, since her pout or 'smouldering eyes' were judged superior to mine.

'And she has a deeper cleavage,' said the director.

'True. She was attacked once by a Viking with an axe.'

After day one, we walked the few hundred yards through a deluge to her family's large modern town-house, sharing her umbrella. She hung up my mack and shook her black leather coat. 'Leather isn't properly waterproof. Rain just soaks through it.'

Her father was a professional conductor and as we sat in the breakfast-room we heard him playing odd excerpts on the baby grand, as he analysed and notated a score.

Chloë brewed tea and toasted some tea-cakes.

'Did that Alwyn eventually take the plunge?'

'Oh, gosh. I invited him round for tea twice, but he seemed depressed and even touching one another didn't feel right. I said to him, "Can't you try to be kind and cheerful?"'

'So just an impasse?'

'Then in Leeds one night, he became drunk and told

his pals that he hated me ... that I was spoilt and had everything. One girl there though was an old school friend and she told me.'

'Oh well ... at least you found out.' Osric flashed into my mind. 'Is there anyone else?'

She reddened a little. 'I'm seeing that M.P. we met, Graham Foy.'

'Oh? That could be exciting. V.I.P. parties?'

'Cross fingers ... and toes.'

Graham would be nearly twice her age.

As I spread honey on my tea-cakes, a porcelain dancing girl stood at one end of the table looking on. 'She's so lovely, youthful ... gay. Eighteenth-century?'

'I think so. Capo di Monte, but not special. Anyway, do you know the director Angus Robertson?'

'No.'

'Well neither did I, but he's planning a film called *A Surfeit of Devils* and it's a sort of sequel to *Ultra-Girl*.'

'Sort of?'

'Well set back in the nineteen-twenties. Anyhow, my agent put me in touch with him and he took me out to lunch.'

'Oh.'

'Of the originals, only Zoë is on board. Eleanor's declined and Fiona has some long-term illness, so he's considering asking us two to replace them ... with you as Charis?'

'I'm flattered.'

'Well ... there's a rub. It's to be a low-budget production.' She smiled. 'Our fees would just be a share of the profits.'

'If there are any?'

'Half a per cent apiece for you and me. Anyway, I'll keep you posted.'

'Thanks.' I gave a dimpled half-grin. 'I have though to complete my final year at Newcastle.'

'Filming's still a long way off, so we'll see. Charis is a courier who … '

'A currier? As in one who dresses and dyes leather?' I teased.

'No,' she grinned. 'Nor the one who prepares your chicken tikka masala.'

It had gone ten and we had to be at the hotel again by seven, so we said good night.

Thinking of this envy-centred Alwyn, I made a fuss of Osric, bought him a course of driving lessons and also a moped, on which – on his free days – he went out to work on our railway station.

We bought a battered short or twenty-foot shipping container, which we could lock to keep any tools or easily stolen items in.

Osric began on a wide sixty-yard driveway; digging it out, edging it with square stone blocks from the collapsed goods shed and then placing in it the reinforced steel meshes before nine inches of concrete were poured and screeded. It included curve-outs where it joined the lane and was a neat job. I was pleased. He then built two wide squat brick gate-posts – though his bricklaying was a touch skewed – before starting to renew or mend all the rail-and-post or post and pig-netting fences.

Occasionally I joined him and shovelled broken tiles into a skip or knocked down the old rotten rafters,

'So, he's back in hospital?'

'Yes. On the coronary care unit.'

We thanked her and wished her well, as she patted Osric on the back and took her leave.

One of Sennacherib's cohorts – gleaming in purple and gold – had been smitten by the angel of the Lord.

We were wholly unsure about the dilapidated railway station. The spot had a profound, almost mystical effect and was not too isolated, there being two villages nearby. The work required though was beyond our reserves or ability. 'A mammoth task.'

'Not a mammoth tusk?'

My beloved looked to be on the up and there had been no further epileptic or febrile episodes.

That night we were together again in Otterburn Terrace, in my bed which had sufficient width and a proper mattress and springs. I was on a period, but we pressed ourselves tightly together, such that I could feel his penis against me. He was asleep, but suddenly I felt his sticky ejaculate through my night-dress. I smiled and stoked him. A second if less earthly joy was – as the stoical, diligent and oppressed Jeremiah had also known – that sense that 'The Lord is with me as with a dread warrior.' Soon *they* would fear *me*.

Claude took Osric on again for three days a week and I began to tackle Anglo-Saxon. I needed to finish my degree, if only to make job-finding easier – as a librarian or whatever – afterwards.

A letter from Social Services said that I should return any material I had, which had come from Fraser's house so that it could be restored to its owner.

Sophie eyed it. 'You see that this is a trap? To do that would show that either you are the thief or that you have received stolen goods.'

'They say I have to reply within fourteen days.' I handed her the Manila envelope.

'Of course you don't. It's only a letter. It's not something serious like a parking fine. And make sure you hide all that stuff safely at your parents ... under some floorboards in the attic for instance.'

At Alnmouth, one sunny bright day, Osric and I paddled in the sea and held hands. It seemed perfect ... unlike Thailand.

'Perhaps Farmer Cowley has now mown his grass for silage?'

Yet there were frictions under the surface. As we grow up and change, skirmishes and adjustments are necessary, though at night we forgot them and floated away into some distant Milky Way, one where dusty comets slid passively by and the universe seemed starry and balmy; glinting, harmless and eternal.

I spoke to Daddy about the station for which there was of course no possibility of a mortgage. He had some bank shares he was willing to sell which would give us about fifteen thousand pounds.

The auction was attended by a few curious locals and ourselves.

The reserve was £15,000. We chose to roll the dice and bid up to £18,000, but as it happened, were the only bidders.

In a short medieval comedy, *Elinor of Cleves*, I played Lady Clare de Baddesey; one-scene and four spoken lines. I wore a mustardy-yellow robe, a white linen wimple and a wooden pectoral cross. 'You're chiefly there for ornamentation,' explained the producer. 'Start by being shy and endearing ... but gradually become more puckish and sceptical.'

This earned just seven hundred and twenty pounds after deducting Terry's cut, but money – though not previously my main emphasis – did now play a *rôle*. It just is a part of modern life. We are no longer Anglo-Saxon serfs, where silver pennies would have no practical use.

Two days later a repair bill came for the Panda which together with four new tyres and a complete exhaust set-up came to seven hundred and twenty pounds. Is there a proverb about the world consisting of circles?

Then Chloë rang. A ladies' fashion house needed two girls to model for their up-market on-line catalogue. Her mother was the assistant director. 'You're a size twelve?'

'Yes.'

'And I'm a ten, so that makes the pairing Mamma says they want. Two strenuous days for two thousand pounds?'

'Oh Chloë, thank you so much.'

'Now Mary, you know that nothing is ever pure goodness. There's something else?'

'Oh?'

'I'll tell you over our next pasta dish.'

Rob came round. 'The police, recognising Fraser as the one who shoved their young female colleague into the bushes, charged him with "assaulting a police officer", but the Prosecution Service have rejected it as "unsafe".'

'Why?'

'Fraser declined to be interviewed, citing ill health. The police girl and I had only seen him in the dark and later identified him from photographs; so not an identity parade. His "attack" on you was dismissed as "unproven" and lastly it was considered "not in the public interest" to undermine confidence in the social services. Summary; the chain of evidence lacks coherence and is therefore unsound.'

I had never really been bitter. My life had been spent, after all, mostly among the upright and fair-minded, yet I was starting to despise these public servants who seemed invariably to shield one another.

An Anglo-Saxon prose piece about a 'witenagemot' – where the chiefs sat on a bench to hear the more serious legal cases – showed a very different spirit.

These wights sought the stability of society and handed out severe penalties to anyone threatening it. Anyone suspected of lies, cop-outs or double-talk, they would come down on heavily.

The door-bell rang.

A police officer stood there of some seniority. He bore no collar number but instead had silver crowns on his epaulettes with red inlays and a silver whistle chain running to the left breast pocket of his jacket.

'Miss Mary Fleet?'

'Yes. Inspector ...?'

'Superintendent Lightfoot.'

I led the way upstairs and we sat down.

He started with a few basic questions, as he sought to establish whether I was sensible or screw-ball. I thought this quite shrewd.

'We are investigating a break-in to the home of the social worker, David Fraser and your name has been put forward as a suspect.'

I took a deep breath. 'One, I do not know where he lives and two, I would not know how to break into a house ... nor have the courage.'

He gave a slow nod. 'You could have asked a professional to do it for you?'

I pretended to think for a few seconds. 'Even if that crossed my mind, I would not know how to find such a person.'

Another thoughtful nod, then a faint smile. 'Have you any suggestions as to who might be behind it?'

'Well, if he goes round spreading wicked and scurrilous stories, then any of his targets?'

'Hmm.'

'Given his criminal and psychopathic tendencies, you do not think that he might have done it himself?'

He smiled a little more warmly. 'Those who do such usually smash up pictures, urinate on the carpet ... that sort of thing, which a straight burglar would not.'

I shook my head slightly.

He stood up, wished me well and I showed him out.

I perched Titus on my knees. 'Do you remember Guy Fawkes, rolling barrels of gunpowder under the citadel?'

He nodded.

'These town-hall crooks by their deceits are betraying the fragile civilisation handed down to us.' I kissed him. 'Shall I be a pagan priestess and cast a slow-burning curse on this marriage of demons?'

Using one of the library's computers, I researched the

names of nine senior town-hall officials, five councillors and two local M.P.s, printed off address labels and stuck them onto stiffened A4 envelopes. I chose eight of the shots I had taken in Fenham, printed each one sixteen times – whilst wearing gloves and on new unopened stationery – then fed them through the printer again to add the caption, 'David Fraser's padlocked second bedroom.' I drove out to Shiremoor to post them.

The fashion shoot took place in a hotel in Harrogate.

Chloë did the lingerie, since her pout or 'smouldering eyes' were judged superior to mine.

'And she has a deeper cleavage,' said the director.

'True. She was attacked once by a Viking with an axe.'

After day one, we walked the few hundred yards through a deluge to her family's large modern town-house, sharing her umbrella. She hung up my mack and shook her black leather coat. 'Leather isn't properly waterproof. Rain just soaks through it.'

Her father was a professional conductor and as we sat in the breakfast-room we heard him playing odd excerpts on the baby grand, as he analysed and notated a score.

Chloë brewed tea and toasted some tea-cakes.

'Did that Alwyn eventually take the plunge?'

'Oh, gosh. I invited him round for tea twice, but he seemed depressed and even touching one another didn't feel right. I said to him, "Can't you try to be kind and cheerful?"'

'So just an impasse?'

'Then in Leeds one night, he became drunk and told

his pals that he hated me ... that I was spoilt and had everything. One girl there though was an old school friend and she told me.'

'Oh well ... at least you found out.' Osric flashed into my mind. 'Is there anyone else?'

She reddened a little. 'I'm seeing that M.P. we met, Graham Foy.'

'Oh? That could be exciting. V.I.P. parties?'

'Cross fingers ... and toes.'

Graham would be nearly twice her age.

As I spread honey on my tea-cakes, a porcelain dancing girl stood at one end of the table looking on. 'She's so lovely, youthful ... gay. Eighteenth-century?'

'I think so. Capo di Monte, but not special. Anyway, do you know the director Angus Robertson?'

'No.'

'Well neither did I, but he's planning a film called *A Surfeit of Devils* and it's a sort of sequel to *Ultra-Girl*.'

'Sort of?'

'Well set back in the nineteen-twenties. Anyhow, my agent put me in touch with him and he took me out to lunch.'

'Oh.'

'Of the originals, only Zoë is on board. Eleanor's declined and Fiona has some long-term illness, so he's considering asking us two to replace them ... with you as Charis?'

'I'm flattered.'

'Well ... there's a rub. It's to be a low-budget production.' She smiled. 'Our fees would just be a share of the profits.'

'If there are any?'

'Half a per cent apiece for you and me. Anyway, I'll keep you posted.'

'Thanks.' I gave a dimpled half-grin. 'I have though to complete my final year at Newcastle.'

'Filming's still a long way off, so we'll see. Charis is a courier who … '

'A currier? As in one who dresses and dyes leather?' I teased.

'No,' she grinned. 'Nor the one who prepares your chicken tikka masala.'

It had gone ten and we had to be at the hotel again by seven, so we said good night.

Thinking of this envy-centred Alwyn, I made a fuss of Osric, bought him a course of driving lessons and also a moped, on which – on his free days – he went out to work on our railway station.

We bought a battered short or twenty-foot shipping container, which we could lock to keep any tools or easily stolen items in.

Osric began on a wide sixty-yard driveway; digging it out, edging it with square stone blocks from the collapsed goods shed and then placing in it the reinforced steel meshes before nine inches of concrete were poured and screeded. It included curve-outs where it joined the lane and was a neat job. I was pleased. He then built two wide squat brick gate-posts – though his bricklaying was a touch skewed – before starting to renew or mend all the rail-and-post or post and pig-netting fences.

Occasionally I joined him and shovelled broken tiles into a skip or knocked down the old rotten rafters,

climbing a ladder and standing high up on the walls to gently wield the sledge-hammer. I also submerged and soaked the new fencing posts in a bath of Solignum, a proprietary brand of preservative creosote. I actually like donkey work ... in moderation.

Our meadow might one day have sweet-scented hay in it or in winter, that nearby stately pine-clad slope would be icy-blue, aglow with the effulgent rays of a low reticent white sun.

An abandoned light Japanese van appeared.

Thieves had forced the lock on the container and loaded into this van our six one-hundredweight bags of Blue Circle cement, before adding a hundred or more bricks, when the floor had given way and the torn bags had spilled their grey powder, forming a heap which embedded the van's rear axle and transmission. Unable to free it, they had removed its number plates and fled.

We had no more spare money and so were limited to clearing the debris and scything and burning undergrowth. Outdoor work though brings a lightness to your heart. You feel you are building on rock and not on sand.

The outline script of *A Surfeit of Devils* came in the post, loosely bound in grey cardboard. I showed it to Osric. 'You do trust me, don't you?'

'Yes Mary, I do.'

'It might bring in some money ... though it's a bit of a gamble.'

He nodded but I could see that deep down, he was not wholly at ease. 'Can you not be a little more manic, a little brighter in spirit?'

He stared at me.

I thought on and off of Mandy and wished we could do something for her.

I had told no one of my untitled letters. I doubted that those uncouth and hard-nosed cynics would give a toss. They could though perhaps be irked or slightly embarrassed, as in war an enemy submarine lurking off your coast is a bit of an unknown quantity.

CHAPTER NINETEEN

A nip appeared in the early mornings and the first orange and yellow leaves floated down from the trees.

The autumn term had begun and its routine was very welcome after the summer's upheavals.

I tried to put David Fraser and his bosses – who were either complicit or bent on shielding him – out of my mind, though their graceless and bare-faced lies still rankled from time to time.

'Sophie, you do know that we are both total idiots, struggling with languages which are such tough nuts?'

'That's the fun.' She pushed me off the sofa. I fought back and we started tickling one another and rolling around on the floor. I stress again that we are not Lesbians, but it is so pleasant and mind-freeing to do such occasionally. After ten minutes of it, moist with sweat, we stood up.

'A psychologist, if he saw us, would be "worried" or "saddened".'

The door-bell rang.

I went down, opened the door and faced two quite smartly dressed men and one woman.

Beyond them the air was crisp, the church spire gaunt, the street calm; such a beautiful, unsullied world.

They showed me their social services I.D. tags.

'Miss Mary Fleet?'

'Yes.'

'May we come in?'

'No.'

'We understand that a number of odd things have happened around here ... people loitering suspiciously for instance? And that this has disturbed you?'

'Well I haven't seen anything odd and I've lived here for two hundred and twenty years.' I had heard this joke the day before.

'We are quite concerned for your well-being Mary. A psycho-analyst has made a tentative *in absentia* diagnosis that you lack metanoia.'

'Metanoia?' I wrinkled my forehead. '"Meta" is "with" and "noos" is "mind"?' I tried to approach it etymologically. 'So I am "without a mind"?'

'I think clinically it has a narrower or more specific meaning.'

'Which is?'

'He said your woodenness suggested "thought block".'

'Which is?'

'A dearth of neurodiversity, perhaps?'

I rolled my eye-balls.

'To move on, a number of anonymous envelopes have been received ... which we think perhaps you may have sent?'

'Oh? What about?'

'They refer allegedly – and we believe falsely – to the pastimes of one of our staff.'

'Can you be less vague?'

'No, but I suspect that you know what we are talking about.'

I shook my head. I knew that Sophie would be listening at the top of the stairs.

'Personal and private matters – such as these – are neither your concern nor ours.'

'Then why are you here?'

'We are seeking a court injunction such that if the professional standing of this employee is again sullied, it will count as contempt of the court.'

'If you can trace the blackguard?'

'Correct.'

'You have though limitless funds for investigatory or legal battles?'

'We have to defend our reputation.'

'What?'

'We can't simply be abused by wrong-headed lunatics.'

'What?'

'Sorry, I'm suffering from an echo here.'

'Perhaps it's bouncing off the inside of your skull?'

After a pause, the spokesman concluded with, 'Well Miss Fleet, this is meant to be a gentle warning … and I hope you will accept it as such. Good day to you.'

I closed the door.

Upstairs, Sophie whispered, 'They were quite high-level. A step up from the usual slobs.'

'Good quality overcoats, anyway.'

She lowered her voice. 'Did you send round copies of those pictures?'

I nodded.

'The obvious move … when they just closed down your uncle.'

We gazed out of the window. A curvaceous blonde was delivering a top-end sports car to a Chinese student across the road.

'Does she come with it?' asked Sophie.

'Rob says he's only had three driving lessons, but his dad is some Party high-up in China ... where money means nothing.'

'What's your next step?'

I looked at her. 'Take my time, think ... ask you.'

Later I recalled a photograph in Fraser's hoard. The originals were in Devon, but I had some copies here in a folder under my bedroom carpet under my bed.

This set of seven photos included four which were plain black and two which were very faint and shadowy.

I showed Sophie the good one. 'This is the woman at the door.'

'Square, Polaroid ... taken at dusk?'

I thought the distance and some encroaching foliage suggested it had been taken covertly.

'Yes, possibly. And with the flash turned off?'

A woman – seen sideways on – sat astride a rough jagged-topped stone wall wearing a belted purple leather coat, a mauve woolly hat and gloves and black leather boots. She was leaning forwards in a jockey-like pose, with her hands gripping a tall wooden post and her legs bent backwards at the knees.

'In *Ultra-Girl*, Ceres climbs over a wall in a raid on a farm, I remember.'

'Or is she stimulating herself?'

'I don't know. I've never done it.'

'Well neither have I,' said Sophie tartly, 'but use some imagination.'

I took a deep breath.

'She would though presumably only want to if there

were something inside her?'

I thought for a moment. 'Could this be Fatso's hold over her?'

'I doubt it. They would stick together anyway ... this lying bunch.'

'In case it's your neck on the block next week?'

'Oh, by the way, when we go out tonight, I want you to tell a lie.'

'Should I post this picture too ... anonymously?'

Sophie shook her head. 'No.'

'I've had the baptism of fire – that first dose of real combat – after which fear disappears.'

She gripped my right upper arm. 'Mary, you're in a strong position. Don't overplay your hand.'

This sounded like tempered, sensible advice.

At seven, we set off for *The Admiral Collingwood* with Sibylle, whose twenty-second birthday it was.

Twilight crept over the roof-tops as we walked to the ivy-clad hostelry and joined Céline, Ed, Yvonne, Gisela and her brother Uwe.

A folk duet – a guitarist and a young Irish lass – were singing *A Bunch of Thyme*.

'Three cheers for the "Kraut",' said Ed.

We all clapped.

'What is this word "Kraut"?' asked Sibylle.

None of us knew.

'I do not understand the English.'

'Few people do.'

Sophie went to the bar to order.

'Has that Fraser oaf bothered you again?' I asked Gisela.

'No. He daren't.'

Yvonne struggled to pun using the word 'chagrin'.

'With his balloon popped, he settled for that Denise.'

'Similar pheromones?'

'Mary,' Yvonne asked with seeming carelessness, 'did Sophie go out last night?'

I pretended to think. 'Er, no ... she stayed in. We tested one another on substantives ... accidence.'

We all listened to *The Rose of Tralee*; such an adorable tune.

I felt pleasantly detached. Often students are trying too hard to establish themselves, to forge an identity.

Sophie returned. 'The pasta's off, so she suggested we fall back on the pies ... but that didn't sound like a good idea.'

'Not pizzas?' Céline cavilled. 'They're so salty here. They shrivel your eye-balls.'

'Making your vision even more skewed?'

'So, it's chicken wings, chips, cheese sauce and mushy peas.'

Uwe was second officer on a small cruise ship, currently tied up down at the Quayside. He was quite sun-burnt – red not charred – having just returned from The Gold Coast.

'Where next?' I asked.

'The Antarctic, calling at Cherbourg, Gibraltar and Saint Helena.'

Gisela's Ph.D. grant required her to link the reduced areas where *Saxifraga collina* is found – wet stony ground – to climate change.

'What if that's not the case?'

'Then you have to warp the results. Today politics calls the tune.'

'So the era of enlightened science has gone?'

'Oh absolutely.'

'Which is why we're into fantasy films,' remarked Ed.

Two girls brought eight platters of chicken wings with their extras.

'I hope they make a second *Ultra-Girl* film,' Céline mused.

'They might, but it's only speculation at present,' I said.

'I love Zoë Sims,' Ed purred.

'How do *you* know about this new film?' Céline chafed.

'Because I might be in it.'

She looked irritated. 'I wish I could be in a film.'

Despite her left-wing views, she displayed odd hankerings for 'grandiosity'. She could also be quite class-conscious over her school and her home in Guildford.

'Prof Jones says you're "very pretty". I would be offended if he said that to me. It makes you sound like a shepherdess.'

'It's just his era. It doesn't upset me. I quite fancy being a shepherdess ... a shepherdess of Arcady.'

Ed mentioned a bribery scandal in his home town. 'The council's first gambit is inaction ... they hope it will go away.'

Céline added, 'Then if it doesn't, they treat the litigant like that mad Miss Flite in *Bleak House*.'

Sibylle said, 'Often these people start quite well, they cut red tape and get things done, but then they go too far and think they can ride over everything. If dictators were limited to a three-year span in office, it might be fine.'

She had acquired cold feet over her medical course. 'The work is relentless ... and my school friends, now lawyers or teachers, are enjoying such cultured and affluent lives.'

'Is it too late to change?' asked Sophie.

'My cousin – three years older than myself – owns a business hiring out cranes ... he's worth millions.'

As I formed my lips into a small 'o' to suck the straw in my juice, Uwe said that he hoped I had been about to kiss him.

I gave him a cutely barbed smile.

Aside from her Ph.D., Gisela gave violin lessons and worked in a bar, yet still had substantial debts.

I went to buy the next round of drinks and she came to help carry them.

Waiting at the bar, I said, 'Are there any jobs going on your brother's ship?'

'For you?'

'No. A girl who's eighteen, a bit simple and gullible and in rehab recovering from drugs ... but she's not a bad girl.'

'They have just lost some people, but ... '

'A job in the galley or something?'

She shook her head slowly. 'She sounds a bit doubtful?'

'I know it's a long shot, but I will vouch for her and ... some money is available if she could be found a post.'

'How much?'

We ordered.

'A thousand pounds?'

She took a deep breath. 'I'll talk to him.'

What a sordid conversation.

A song about a Belfast lad fondling his girl behind the gas works was in full swing. A British Army armoured car suddenly appeared and turned its lights on them.

'Well, a new kind of climax for them,' remarked Ed.

So an evening of ups and downs, but the next day I found myself making a frantic round trip to Carlisle. The rehab staff were very obstructive, but they could not legally hold Mandy and luckily she trusted me. We went to a hairdresser's, I gave her a smart burgundy pinafore dress and my new black woollen coat and so – in the early evening – she went aboard the cruise ship *Persephone*.

The hired bramble-destroying giant-propeller-fitted tractor came on a day when Osric had a hospital outpatient appointment, so I spent hours driving it round our field, doing a thorough job and clearing each corner and going close up to each boundary; a number-one hair-cut.

Afterwards, Jim Cowley promised to put some cows onto it to keep the brambles and weeds down. There was a small stream on the far side from which they could drink.

I wandered round our rime-frosted railway station as an icy breeze wafted gently down from the north.

I thought of Gisela with her retorts, her predetermined experimental conclusions and the betrayal of the privileges and freedoms established by our more classically educated predecessors.

Grass and stones and the glimpse of a redstart did more for my spirit than such supposedly high-flying knowledge. Basic Latin or elementary French too say, have a solid or more tangible appeal than the denser and often ill-grounded clever stuff.

That evening Osric said, 'Mary, you have such lovely parents, a liberal education, such a superfluity of everything … all at the drop of a hat?'

I lay across his lap. 'We all have things we wish were different. I would love to be more musical, but I just have no natural ability. When I was seven I started piano lessons, but after two years the teacher said to my father that I was wasting her time and his money.'

'But you still have three aces out of four?'

'Your family's error is that they don't try to make things happen. They think it's about money, but that's an illusion.'

I sat up and kissed him, but there was no response.

As with Chloë's Alwyn, was there a hint of jealousy or a touch of resentment there at the low-value cards – as he saw it – which he had been dealt?

Still, Osric was occupied at work mostly with the Albion lorry's restoration and I was engrossed with my three final-year subjects. We were both industrious and painstaking with our tasks.

One cold quiet night in early December, at about a half past two, Osric and I were asleep when Sophie – who had worked late on an essay and only just climbed into bed – heard someone at the front door. She came and shook us.

'Keep quiet, but there's someone at the front door.'

We stood up and pulled on some pullovers since it was so cold.

Sophie peered down the stairwell. 'I think they're trying to push a bank card between the door and the frame to ease back the catch.'

Then, glimpsed in the thin glow of a street-light, she saw Fatso enter with a pistol and a holdall.

'God,' she whispered, 'we'll try to spring on him as he comes into your room.'

We sweated and waited in the deep shadows on either side of my bedroom door. We heard the stairs creak, then a floor-board. Then he appeared, but slowly and cautiously and he stopped just short of the doorway such that our plan to jump on him fell flat.

Perhaps he glimpsed our outlines in the gloom or he sensed our breathing, for he dropped the holdall and took a step to his right. He must then have spotted either Osric or myself to the left of the doorway, aimed the pistol and fired.

The first bullet struck Osric's right forearm and the second his right flank. I struggled to pull us both down onto the floor.

A few seconds later, a third bullet went into the woodwork as Sophie tried to grapple with him and although he threw her aside, his pistol fell to the floor and she managed to kick it such that it spun off under the bed.

Fatso paused and glared into the darkness before leaving like some slow-moving macabre spectre. There followed an horrendous clatter, then a nerve-jangling squeal as he fell down the stairs.

I knelt, holding my lover from behind, as he fainted and sank.

Sophie turned my desk-lamp on and in the holdall found a wedding dress and a bottle of champagne.

Others woke up. Rob, Julian and Sibylle were there within four or five minutes.

Soon the street was abuzz with six or seven emergency vehicles.

Fraser, in a crumpled heap beside the open front door had a pulse and was breathing, but seemed unable to move. An ambulance crew took him away. Osric, although faint and groggy, also had a pulse and was breathing and looked not to have any life-threatening injuries.

I allowed him to be taken from my grasp, but went with him to the hospital, where I found myself sitting in bleak corridors for most of the night.

Sophie had removed the magazine and the bullet in the firing-chamber from the pistol and photographed it. She said later that it was quite antiquated and of an unusually large bore.

As a cock crowed and the first glimmers of dawn broke the eastern sky, the last policemen left and some reporters rolled up.

Sophie told them of my defamation by the social services, but despite pretending to be interested, they were not going to blacken those with such influence and power. They ignored what she said and just printed a few bare facts.

Osric went to theatre. The flank wound had to be

opened so that the bullet track could be cleaned to prevent infection. In his right forearm the bullet had passed between the ulna and the radius, but that too had to be cleaned and tidied up and the severed median nerve and a tendon repaired.

I have never inquired of Sophie how it came about that Fatso fell down the stairs, but I am pretty sure I know.

His broken neck left him tetraplegic. Broken at the level between the fourth and fifth cervical vertebrae, the spinal cord had been trapped and crushed there. Sibylle has explained that unlike peripheral nerves, spinal nerves do not regenerate and so he was left paralysed and without sensation from the neck down. Since however the nerve roots which supply the diaphragm leave the spinal cord at the three levels above this, he could breathe unaided.

I had a vivid dream the next afternoon. I grabbed Fatso's hair, tipped his head back and it came off. Blood flowed everywhere.

Judith, in the Apocrypha, had in her finest clothes gone to the tent of the Greek commander Holophernes, cut his head off and carried it by the hair back into her own besieged town.

Osric came to me too and I said to him, 'Don't bury your head in the sand my love. You are worth so much to me.'

The court-submitted injunction was withdrawn before going before a judge. The social services did not offer me 'support' nor supply the usual 'useful telephone numbers'.

The senior ward sister had penned a rescission of the Kardex entry. Her account of her 'misunderstanding' was both convoluted and clumsy. Since she did not work in social services, they could not force her to lie, so what pressure had they brought to bear?

I said to Sophie, 'The road to the land flowing with milk and honey was never easy.'

'We're doing all right,' she replied, then taking my hands quoted the Iliad. 'A rose-fingered morn, the daughter of dawn, displayed in her light the enemy's plight.'

CHAPTER TWENTY

I had expected to spend Christmas with Osric at home in Devon. Mummy had even discreetly asked me if he would like to sleep in my bed? This though was not to be.

Sophie and I had each received a letter from a 'victim support agency' offering to arrange a visit by a psychologist.

I tore mine in half, but Sophie accepted. 'I'm just curious. What is this "counselling" they offer?'

'It's an official outfit. You don't think they might report back to social services?'

'Don't they have to maintain confidentiality?'

'Well, it's not medical is it? Not a psychiatrist?'

'Anyway, I don't intend to give anything away.'

Four days later Sophie asked if I wanted to sit in her room and eavesdrop. 'But don't cough or laugh.'

She had on her black leather mini-skirt, frilly white blouse and some dabs of her favourite purple-and-pink make-up.

'What are you thinking of doing?'

'I'm not sure ... but aren't these people all sex-obsessed?'

'Well, tell him – or her – that life is really about cups of tea ... though in that get-up it might not wash.'

Dr Chadwick, early forties and bespectacled was apparently quite conventional in his dress and demeanour.

Sophie sat him down, smiled and offered him tea, which he accepted.

Whilst he broke the ice – as he imagined – and outlined the relief he hoped to offer, she boiled the kettle and found some biscuits. This 'expert' lacked buoyancy or *joie de vivre*. He actually sounded depressed.

'This episode must be quite worrying for you, I imagine?'

'Not really. A biscuit?'

'But the shock of having to face an armed intruder? Perhaps it has not struck home yet? Our minds can be in denial ... but that too is not healthy. Its effects can erupt later?'

'The failed killer was a social worker?'

'Yes, unfortunately ... an odd black sheep seems to have slipped through the wire.'

'His bosses say he is highly esteemed and works to the highest ethical standards.'

Chadwick exhaled. 'I suppose they cannot know everything about their employees' private lives?'

I could imagine Sophie smiling.

'It is often good to talk a little about some happier part of your life. How would you describe your childhood?'

'Unspectacular ... but generally fairly happy.'

'That's good. That's positive. Psychiatrists say we are formed and fixed in our natures by the time we are twenty-one ... well some even put it as low as sixteen.'

'My flat-mate says they underestimate the possibilities of release ... or redemption. She cites Mary of Magdala, Peer Gynt, Saul of Tarsus.'

'Hmm. Does she study psychology?'

'No. Languages and history.'

'Oh ... is she the actor?'

'An actress ... on and off, yes.'

'We're not supposed to say "actress" now ... It's proscribed. It has a sexual bias.'

'Oh?'

'Some committee for gender equality has listed it as forbidden.'

'On whose authority?'

'Well, their own I guess.'

'So it's not law?'

'Er ... probably not. Anyway, shall we perhaps leave that diversion and focus on the effects this episode has had on your own mental well-being? I am here to help you personally ... not to discuss world affairs.' He gave an awkward little laugh.

'Oh?'

'Are you having nightmares or has this dreadful event changed your composure or outlook?'

'No. Do you like my skirt?'

Sophie said later that she had seen his trouser-fronts stir as he began to have an erection.

'Your skirt? Well, I hadn't noticed ... but, yes it does make you look quite attractive ... or perhaps I should say even *more* attractive.'

'It's starting to become skewed and misshapen ... but men often seem to like it ... so a good investment, wouldn't you agree?'

'Well ... then I suppose so.'

'My flat-mate thinks it's a bit vulgar. She says a knee-length one, flared and with neatly sewn pockets would be more tasteful.'

He grinned uneasily. 'I think I would beg to differ.'

'Anyway, as you can see ... I am more or less over my troubles, so thank you for coming, but I'll be all right.'

'Well, no, that's good news indeed. We have to "move on" as the saying is ... but some people do become stuck.'

'Yes.'

As they stood up, he hesitated. 'Forgive me if I am saying something I shouldn't, but ... you wouldn't like to meet on a *less formal* occasion would you?'

'No thank you.' She smiled and showed him out.

'And what was the point of that?' I asked.

'I don't know ... but are these people doing anything at all?' She put her hands on my shoulders. 'Mary, is it my turn to apologise?'

I thought briefly. 'No. I don't think so.'

'Keep an eye on me.'

'I'll try,' I smiled.

'On a six-figure salary, for that crap? And my cheerful little cousin works so hard in a tinned-soup factory for a pittance.'

The next day Sibylle came up at lunch-time and asked me down to share bacon butties with her. This seemed a little odd, especially at midday, but I obliged.

'White rolls,' she declared proudly.

'You're learning. Bacon *only* goes with white bread.'

'Do you want some devil's claw tea?'

'No thanks.'

'It is quite bitter ... and smells like urine.'

'My mother had an old German herbal book. Someone had written on it, "*Germania contra mundum*".'

'Crazy,' Sibylle shook her head. 'But those days are

gone luckily. No one's a hundred per cent German anyway. My great-grandfather was born in German East Africa, where his father was an engineer but his mother was an Indian housemaid. Then I had a great-grandmother who was Persian ... though of course "Iranian" is the same word as "Aryan" isn't it?'

'I'm not the ultimate source of knowledge on such things.'

I had a feeling that she was just talking for the sake of it and so eventually I excused myself, as I intended to visit Osric in an hour.

She took my arm to prevent my standing up. 'Mary, I have something to tell you.'

'Oh?'

'Do you know where Sophie is?'

'No.'

'She's gone to see Osric.'

'What? Why?'

'She asked me to keep you occupied. She had a telephone call from him. He says he never wants to see you again.'

I was too stunned to speak.

After a couple of minutes, she asked, 'Do you want a brandy?'

'No thanks.'

I went upstairs and looked at the ceiling for about an hour. Oddly I felt very little; no anger, no fury, no hurt. Was I reaping what I had sown? Yet I had not been building on sand, had I?

Sophie appeared.

'Is it true?'

'Yes.'

'Did he say why?'

She wore baggy dark trousers and a greenish woolly. She made tea, munched a cheese and celery bun and did not reply.

After prompting, she sat beside me and took my hand. 'He's "in love" with his physiotherapist.' After a pause, she added, 'She came whilst I was there.'

'And?'

'I didn't have the impression that there were too many lights on upstairs. Enormous tits though.'

'Did you catch her name?'

'Angela. It was on her badge … which dangled from one of her nipples. Sorry, I didn't mean to hurt you.'

Was I just naïve, too innocent, stupid? Were all these 'live and let live' folk the ones who actually understood things? I thought of Saint John; 'God is light and in Him there is no darkness.' I sniffled and wanted to cry, but could not.

Osric had sometimes bewailed his limited repertoire of interests, but I had said that that could be good. Narrowness of field gives colour, devotion, depth, love … and under-confidence is as harmful as over-confidence.

I visited my tutor to ask if it would be possible to take the rest of the year out and return for my final year in September 2019?

He made tea and we sat down.

'Given the shooting Mary … and this ghastly social worker, there will be no difficulty with that.'

I thanked him quietly, but did not mention the more personal aspect.

'I went to a rather monotonous cricket match recently with a senior colleague,' he began.

'Oh?' I wondered if non-monotonous cricket matches existed? Perhaps those where it is rained off and you can go and do something useful?

'He's delighted by what has happened. His wife became demented and violent and the social services said they could not intervene without a psychiatrist's report ... knowing of course that she would never consent to be assessed. He knew though of a man who had hurt his wife and they took her into care for her own safety, so he said this was sexual discrimination. No reply. He is though good friends with a local M.P., who stirred things up on his behalf. Two junior social workers also said that without doubt his wife needed to be sectioned, but Fraser blocked it. It seems he relished leaving this "trouble maker" in a desperate spot.'

'Revenge for making a complaint?'

'Fraser asked him if he wanted his wife out of the way because he had homosexual tendencies? When he nearly went through the roof, Fraser smirked and said, "The eyes see what the eyes see." This academic realised that Fraser's game was to goad him into some reckless act, so he could then call the police and label him as violent or unstable. Eventually his wife had to go into a care home because of shop-lifting, damaging neighbours' cars, et cetera, but Fraser told the staff at this Elm Tree Croft Care Home that he used to beat her up and must not be allowed any form of contact with her ... '

'Was this verbal?'

'Oh yes, very definitely.'

'That fits ... completely. That's his method and the service seems to have no way or no will to cleanse itself of these bad apples.'

The solicitor rang about the Land Registry form for the station purchase. 'In joint names, you said?'

'No, change that please. Just in my name.'

I was very sorry to leave Sophie, but promised to visit her now and then. 'And I'll be back in September.'

'Yes.'

'I wondered at first if it might just be a late sequela of the encephalitis ... but not so.'

'No.'

'Just that she is more sexy or curvy than I?'

'Aren't men just unbelievable?'

'I just so felt he was the right one ... and still do.'

'Yes ... and there's no accounting for that.'

'Perhaps I have been too sure of myself, my future, my strength, my ability to love and to hold?'

She gave me a kindly yet knowing smile. 'Don't worry. "One door closes and another opens." You'll be all right.'

CHAPTER TWENTY-ONE

Over Christmas I told Mummy everything, including that first encounter with Nick Yates. It rekindled our closeness. She cuddled and consoled me.

'I am not as virtuous as I like to think ... or appear,' I said in a subdued tone.

The first Beatitude 'Blessed are the poor in spirit,' can be paraphrased as 'Blessed are those who know their need of God,' for although the Greek word 'beggar-like' or 'beggarly' might mean 'poor' or 'wretched', it might also signify 'like a beggar' that is 'holding out a begging bowl' and so one who understands their need.

Terry Duffield called. 'Mary, would you like to present two thirty-minute television documentaries?'

'Oh yes. That's something a bit different.'

'Topic; the early history of Ireland.'

'Er ... I can't do an Irish accent?'

'Ah, begorrah.' In London he introduced me to his clients.

I had applied for some clerical jobs and in early January was interviewed successfully for a temporary part-time office-junior post with the West Mercia Constabulary.

It is strange how in retrospect, there is both a rhyme and a reason to the turmoil which at such times engulfs you.

I arrived in Belfast.

A chastened, quiet yet aesthetic air had taken hold of my being, which I think quite suited the more detached *rôle* of narrator.

In *In Irish Pastures*, filmed near the Mountains of Mourne, a coastal village of their early bardic period was depicted. The population of Ireland would then have been less than a million and Brian Boru was their High-King.

Two greenfinches in a copse of evergreens with a silent wintry sun illumining them, formed the opening backdrop as I walked through a patch of valerian and nettles whilst talking. A kneeling, bare-footed peasant girl in a coarse grey woollen dress rolled a rounded stone back and forth on a granite slab to grind corn near a row of low dry-stone huts with thatched roofs. A coracle lay drawn up on the shore, where some nets and herring had been hung up on poles to dry. Colleen, an older girl, played a few strange notes – thin and mournful – on a crudely carved *flûte à bec*.

Afterwards I picked up this replica pipe and imagined myself as the Greek Muse Euterpe … until I tried to play it. I could not get a single note out of it.

In *A Riddle in County Clare* we visited a fortified homestead by an inland waterway. A lady in dyed woollen shawls and sheepskins listened to a rough-clad peasant lad with a clarsach harp singing in Old Gaelic to a plaintive air. The harp was made of oak and willow and had twenty-nine strings. The church in Ireland had in that era been largely monastic with its monks devoted to the study of God's word, to fasting and to manual labour. In a ruined abbey and in a library, those admired artists and scribes who penned the illuminated manuscripts were evoked.

I plucked the strings of the small harp, but musical

talent is definitely a genetic trait and not one I possess.

Though outwardly placid and good-humoured whilst on set, alone in the evenings in a string of hotel rooms, I was quite down. I would never despair – my faith would prevent that – but there was an emptiness in my heart and perhaps my looks were fading?

Also the misdeeds of the 'carer' band-wagon fakes, though you try not to let them affect you, inevitably do.

In some hard-to-define way, I did not feel too good. I sensed that I had lost the glow or purity which I had had during the filming of *The Moroccan Plot*. 'Dejected', was too strong, but I lacked the spontaneity and brightness of only a year before.

As absurd as it seems, on the last evening I actually sat with the script and counted the words I had spoken – eight hundred and ten – so dulled was my spirit.

Terry rang. He had lined up a brief last-minute appearance for me in a television serialisation of the spy novel *Duff Bluff*.

Used to easy triumphs, I wondered if my social service enemies were breathing a cautious sigh of relief? More experienced military commanders though, would know that mopping-up operations can be very bloody and drawn-out.

I reviewed the packet of polaroid photos. On it was written, 'Ridsdale: October 2016.'

Beside the fairly distinct one of Jill sat on the wall, two others displayed dim outlines. In one an older man in Celtic philibegs was atop a huge cloth-made Austrian doll. In the third, a girl was tipping a jug of water over a man's head, rather as Socrates's wife Xanthippe had over the philosopher, whilst he was waffling away in the market-place and she – presumably – thought he should be at home mending the roof. Were they a coven of voyeurs, where each had to do a turn?

I made a copy on glossy photo paper of the one good picture, guillotined it to a five-inch square and stencilled on the back 'Ridsdale: October 2016: shot number 6.' I sent it – again in a stencil-addressed envelope – to Jill Vickerton.

In early February, in the small market town of Evesham, on the northern edge of the Cotswolds, I started my new job; three days a week in its small rural police station.

I had swapped to using my middle name, Una.

I shared an upstairs office with Inspector Laurence Sear, a cordial and imperturbable fellow, who spent much time during my first week explaining my tasks; what to do and more emphatically what not to do.

Our desks were back to back, the chairs hard and wooden and the ceiling still brownish from the days when smoking had been allowed.

My desk was a solid old oak one with a red-leather inset on its top. In the drawers lay an old 'Force Handbook', a dusty copy of 'Moriarty's Police Law', *Biggles Learns to Fly* and a few separate Acts of Parliament which had been sought when a particular case needed closer study. Also were the lipsticks and hair-brushes of the girl whose maternity leave I was covering.

The officers need to feel that they can trust your discretion and impartiality.

On my third day, Inspector Sear said, 'I have to

interview this girl caught spraying a slogan on the T.S.B. Bank. She says she's an "anti-revanchist", whatever that is.'

'Do you know what revanchism is, Sir?'

'No.'

'It's a policy of trying to recover lost territory … as in France after the Franco-Prussian War, when they had lost Lorraine and Alsace.'

'So does she think we're trying to recover the colonies?'

'She probably hasn't a clue … just a word she's repeating.'

'Hmm. I'll see if she knows.'

I had read the charge sheet. 'She claims that the officer arresting her used her baton, but Constable Brightwell denies that.'

'If you draw your baton, you do have to record it. It was near to midnight, so she probably used her torch … you don't have to record that.'

The following week he asked, 'You speak Italian, don't you?'

'Yes, to a degree.'

'Come with me.'

We went downstairs and into an interview room where a tape-recorder stood. He closed the door, inserted a tape and played the first half-minute. 'Do you understand that?'

'Yes, I think so.'

'Settle yourself down will you and write a transcript? One's Giulio di Luzio, but I don't know who the other is.'

Fifteen minutes and a cup of tea later; 'Here you are Sir. The other guy's first name is Marco.'

Giulio: 'Are you on for the Jaguar 'C' tonight?'

Marco: 'Yes, boss.'

Giulio: 'I think the police suspect the dark green container, so don't take it there.'

Marco: 'Got it, boss.'

Giulio: 'Instead take it to the lock-up in Slessford. Have you got keys?'

Marco: 'Yes.'

Giulio: 'I'll be in *The Pheasant*.'

Marco: 'Okay boss. Roger.'

Inspector Sear gave a nod and a smile. 'Una, I wish I could give you a kiss.'

'Perhaps at a party, Sir?'

He held up a photo of Giulio. A striped suit with wide lapels, a Trilby and gold tooth fillings. 'All he needs is a cigar.'

Soon afterwards Odile Beauregard, a buxom French tourist, had seen someone break a jeweller's window. I was asked to sit in on, jot down and then translate parts of her statement.

'The trajectory or parabola of the brick ended when it hit the plate-glass window of Bezant's the Jewellers. In the bright rays of the morning sunshine, thousands of kaleidoscopic patterns were thrown off by the diamonds glittering amid the glass fragments as the man with a slight limp ran off. He wore light-blue jeans and a torn leather jacket with studs and the words "The Helots" stamped on it in light-grey letters.'

The police knew him and brought him in.

His defence lawyer claimed that *someone else* had thrown the brick and that his client – good citizen that he was – was merely tidying up the mess and ensuring that no bad person stole anything.

One lunch-break I wandered up into the High Street. I ate tagliatelle in a cosy little café, then drifted into a charity shop and spotted a leather skirt. It was black, A-line, knee-length and with an elasticated waist. The label said it had been made in Nicosia and it was of a slightly thicker or stiffer leather than the soft goatskin hides then coming into fashion. If Eleanor, Sophie and even perhaps Chloë set such store by these items, then I too would give it a go; and only seven pounds!

Back at the station, the desk sergeant said, 'The Super wants to see you.'

Superintendent Drake, a severe man, sat me down in his office and waved at an inch-thick folder.

'Bill Mead was a sergeant in the Tewkesbury Sub-Division, until he retired, bought *The Jolly Roger* and became a publican.'

I adjusted my pose and crossed my legs, as I could see this would be a long tale.

'He placed a girl named Tracy Titley on his "banned board" for fighting. She was though – unknown to Bill – the council chief executive's floosie.'

I sat poised, pencil tip on my note-pad, but writing nothing down.

'Don't you need to take notes?'

'No, Sir. I can remember this.'

'So, an environmental health officer rolls up and says his ham's mouldy, his peanuts are out of date and the drains are blocked. Various complaints flow in from supposed unhappy customers and the pub is closed.

Bill tried to protest, but was stone-walled at every turn. Are you with this, Una?'

'Absolutely.'

'It had seemed impossible to probe the town-hall's doings, until the chief executive's feisty young assistant secretary, when passed over for a promotion, wrote a five-page letter to Bill telling him how the whole thing had been rigged.'

I had to compile a chronological table in which each incident or alleged incident was listed and then cross-referenced to anything which either supported or refuted it.

It had the codename, 'Operation Galatea'.

During my afternoon tea-break in the little rest-room, Keith Still, the station's vehicle mechanic, strolled in in his oil-smudged blue overalls. They were unbuttoned at the top, showing an inverted delta of hairy chest.

The laconic Sergeant Hines sat at one table, Inspector Lewis – a detective with a small moustache – at another and I at the third.

Perhaps I looked the least formidable?

'May I join you?'

Apart from glimpsing one another, we had not properly met. I rotated my eyeballs upwards and smiled. 'Of course.'

I had dressed nicely each day and had on my blue and red tartan skirt, a white blouse with a little bow at the neck, a navy cardigan and black tights. I had also had my hair cut a little shorter and had it fixed in a French plait which came just a couple of inches below my collar.

'I'm Keith,' he said, whilst blotting up some drips of tea with a paper napkin from the old Formica-topped table.

'Una.'

'I know.' He smiled and gave a wink.

Keith would be in his late twenties, easy-going in a down-to-earth sort of way, tall, with a boyish face and short spiky brown hair ... not unlike Osric.

His knee touched mine. 'Sorry.'

Was this 'brush' intentional? I felt strangely attracted to him. Is there a semi-scientific axiom, 'nature abhors a vacuum'?

'You live at Tie's Gill?'

'Just outside ... in a converted cow-byre.'

'And are you married?' Why for goodness' sake, had I asked that?

'My wife's called Dana.' His dunked biscuit broke off and he fished for the lost half with a teaspoon. 'We're not on good terms though.'

I was a bit surprised by such a confidence, but confined myself to saying, 'I'm sorry.'

'Sorry, I shouldn't have said that.'

'Brats?'

'No.'

'Then ... at least you're not trapped?' Was I in the grip of some demon ventriloquist?

'No. Dana's away at ...' He switched to, 'We

nearly bought the old tithe barn in the village, but the decoration was grotesque.'

'Not Michelangelo then?'

'I don't know. Did he use runny paints and wood filler?'

Inspector Lewis came over. 'I'm sorry to interrupt this rather intimate conversation, but Una, have you processed those E50's?'

'I've done six, Sir. The other three tomorrow.'

He seemed satisfied, smiled and left.

I left at ten past five. My car was in the compound at the rear of the station. The sun shone softly and obliquely and beyond the wire fence lay a cabbage field where rabbits frolicked.

Keith spent most of his time in the vehicle shed and I could see that he had a Panda car up on the lift and was busy underneath it. I folded up a plaid and a headscarf, which lay tossed on my back seat, then tidied up some bottles of oil and screen-wash in the luggage space at the back.

Suddenly he was there. 'Una ... would you like to come and watch a film this evening?'

I tried to look surprised. 'Oh, umm ... er, yes.'

Back in my little rented, modern, end-of-terrace house, I peered in the mirror. I had never felt like this before, sexy, errant and wanting to take my panties off. I had always thought myself above these things.

Jeremiah says; 'You are leaving the straight path and stumbling into crooked ways, for you crave to burn incense to false gods.' I suddenly felt like telling Jeremiah to jump off a cliff. Was I just five years behind everyone else in understanding or acknowledging our bodies' needs or in 'growing up' as you might call it?

I arrived at Keith's grey stone cottage – a little late naturally – at a quarter past eight.

'Are you alone?'

'Yes. My wife's at her mother's in Basingstoke. Come in.'

We kissed, first a peck then a longer mouth-to-mouth kiss with an embrace. My genitals stiffened. Damnation.

He wore work-a-day blue trousers, thick socks and a loose off-white shirt. He ushered me through the kitchen and into a sunken sitting-room. I had on my new second-hand leather skirt, a white T-shirt and a white cardigan. I had a new bra too, with a little bit of shaped padding.

Keith glanced at my small pointed – though not overdone – breasts as they pushed the T-shirt out slightly between the edges of the unfastened cardigan.

This modest single-storey dwelling consisted of five low-ceilinged rooms in a line.

The sitting-room was intimate and warm; one curved sofa, a coffee-table and a large-screen telly; everything to hand ... all it lacked was a sexy girl.

He turned down the lights, brought in two microwaved fish-pie meals and some fizzy apple drink, sat down close beside me and pressed the 'start' button for the film.

The film was *Zeppelin*. Michael York and Elke Sommer were well cast as the leads and both Rupert Davies and the German tailor in their short scenes oozed both naturalness and conviction.

I paid it close attention – at least initially – since

Ultra-Girl 2 was to be set in the period immediately after the First World War.

Yet with nothing said, we were soon touching one another; hands, then thighs, necks and chests.

As we lay horizontally on the sofa, I imagined Chloë in a blue Ionic robe and pink waist-band in scene nine, seducing the French ambassador. I could see her writhing about excitingly with her 'prey'. I was even secretly envious of this fictitious conquest and tried to emulate it now in reality.

By the time the airship had crashed and exploded, our kissing and fondling had become intense.

'Bed?' He asked.

I nodded.

Passing through the utility room, I stubbed my unshod left foot's big toe on a large square carcass structure held by sash cramps.

'I glued it this morning,' he said as I hopped around clutching my foot. 'Those off-cuts are just so that the clamps don't mark the wood. Screw and glue – it'll be strong.'

'Oh?' Screw and goo? Hmm. I eyed the bench, the racks of tools and pieces of wood.

In bed we kissed softly and wetly on each other's lips. He cuddled and kissed my slightly augmented breasts, then put his head under my T-shirt and slobbered into my navel.

I breathed deeply with delight as my now more pointed breasts rose and fell.

I wondered whether to say that he could relieve himself on top of me, like Eleanor in the wood with

Nick. I could sponge his sticky stuff off my leather skirt later and it would serve as an effective contraceptive since I was at the high-risk point, half-way between periods.

He tried to pull it up. 'I think you need to take it off?'

An inescapable dichotomy.

He turned me on my side and started to unzip it.

I took it off

'And your panties.'

I think we did it six times. It was so good, so exquisite and – though I hate to admit it – I seemed almost desperately to need it.

With daybreak, Keith whispered, 'You're the fourth girl I've slept with ... and by gosh, the others weren't a patch on you.'

Whether he meant my looks or the sex was not entirely clear.

The following day I was free. In the morning I showered and felt all right.

I thought of Sibylle, who often seemed so blatantly egocentric, yet was perhaps just being practical and realistic?

Yet as the day wore on, my mind gradually darkened. I felt coarsened in some subtle way. My usual serenity ebbed away. This wild 'adventure' must not happen again. That I knew.

I again compared Sophie and Belinda. One with blithe good intentions, the second I suspected, of harbouring crude or grimy yearnings.

But only Osric mattered. Nothing else did; career, beauty, success. In the evenings I sometimes developed a slight tremor. I wondered if people thought I had aged suddenly?

I opened the second folder we had stolen from Fatso's secret den. Scrawled across two pictures of myself were,' I'm too good for any mere mortal' and 'I'm beautiful, but don't touch'.

A sub-section related to Sibylle.

'Sibylle Anneliese Hauff, born 22 – 10 – 1996.' Her home address was Libellenstrasse 7, Hanover. Her mother – who had absconded when Sibylle was six – lived in Fassberg. Could a tough family life account for her being quite hard-bitten?

There was too, a hand-written letter:

'Delectably shaped Sibylle,

Do Valkyries like sex? Yes, but only in secret. They are not as pure and radiant as they would like us to believe. They have slaves not boyfriends. Can I be your slave? Enchain me in your subterranean cave and let us revel in ceaseless and ecstatic orgasms.

And my delight would be, that you would not let me escape, because if I did the other Valkyries would make fun of you for your weakness. But perhaps I might pretend to attempt to flee, so that you could beat me up and lash me?

Your frenzied Nibelung lover.'

No stencilled or typed copy existed and Sibylle had never mentioned such a letter.

Sobered by my own fall, I saw once more that good and evil, light and darkness, do exist. It is not simply a question of taste or 'where you are coming from'.

I read Isaiah: 'O daughter of the Chaldeans, you shall no longer be called tender and delicate.' Daniel said: 'And that very night, Belshazzar, the Chaldean king was slain.'

Next day as I hung my jacket up in the parade room, Keith appeared and grinned.

I gave him a short cold glance.

After closing his locker door, he brought his knuckles up to touch my elbow. For a second I allowed him to sustain contact, then withdrew suddenly, as if electrocuted.

'I didn't invite that touch.'

He seemed surprised. 'Was it just a one-night affair then?'

'Don't pester me again.'

'I'm sorry.'

'Not as sorry as I am. Oh well ... it happened ... unfortunately.' I danced off, leaving him to ponder my retreating form.

Eating alone in a pub that evening, a girl – three sheets to the wind – sat down opposite me, uninvited.

'You work at the police station, don't you?' she slurred.

'Yes.'

'I'm Violet.'

'Violet Grey?'

She raised her brows. 'Yes. "Violet", lovely name isn't it?'

I eyed her, if not with kindness at least not with unkindness and wondered if her middle name might be 'Scarlet'.

'I can't grass on Darrel O'Keefe ... can I?'

'Violet, I can't discuss police matters.' I looked at her. 'If he is guilty of a criminal act though, it may end up badly.'

She gave me a hard glare, as if to say, 'You're just like the rest of them.'

I said softly yet dispassionately, 'You ought not to shield him ... even if facing up to it is hard?'

She studied my expression for a full ten seconds, then left. On the back of her leather jacket, gold letters spelt 'The Helots'.

A woman, seated alone at the next table, turned towards me. 'Some years back, I used to give her singing lessons ... a quite attractive contralto ... especially for her age.'

'Are you a singing teacher?'

'Yes.' She smiled.

'Do you have a slot for a new pupil?'

'Yes.'

And so I began twice-weekly lessons. I bought a basic electronic keyboard.

One afternoon, Detective Inspector Lewis came to my office.

'Una, we are about to interview a council administrator named Marilyn Hale. She is quite disturbed and her thoughts are very fragmented. She has asked if another female – and not a police officer – could be present ... and we think that's a sensible plan.'

The two officers sat her down and introduced themselves courteously.

'So Marilyn, you've asked to make a statement about illegal activities within the council, we understand?'

'Yes.'

She was forty-two, very evidently agitated and shaking noticeably.

'You seem quite anxious. Would you like to wait a little?'

'No.'

'Or a cup of tea or coffee?'

She nodded vigorously, so Inspector Lewis popped out briefly to arrange this.

'I'm sorry.'

'No, no. That's perfectly all right, Marilyn.'

'I've been prescribed these little blue pills, called SSRI's, for depression, but they make me feel disorientated, panicky ... as if I'm going insane ... as if I want to throw myself under a train.'

'Well,' Superintendent Drake exhaled slowly, 'that is a medical matter. We will ring your family doctor and if they cannot see you, we will ask our police surgeon to come.'

Sitting in the background, it sounded to me as if the cure here was worse than the illness.

With two others, she had received bribes for granting planning permission for two large areas of land.

A junior had threatened to expose her unless she went to bed with him, which she did.

The canteen girl brought in a cup of tea and a gingerbread biscuit.

'Thank you,' she shuddered. 'My mouth is so dry. I think that's the tablets too.'

'Take your time Marilyn,' said the Inspector, as she sipped her tea with a trembling hand.

'God, what a fat oaf. I feel so awful. When Stalin's daughter was pestered by a fat oaf, Pappa sent him to the gulag. Damn the bastard. He looks vile ... as if he's sexually active for fifty per cent of the time.'

She then spoke of her boss, who had also received money into some Luxembourg bank account. 'She's so ugly that he didn't want to shag her. Her virginity's safe.'

The tape-recorder's reels turned silently.

In trying to pick up her cup again, her hand half-missed the handle and some tea was spilt on the table.

'I'm sorry. I've got blurred vision too. These tablets are supposed to lift your spirits, not send you crazy.'

'It doesn't matter Marilyn,' urged the Superintendent.

'I don't think I'm safe to drive.'

'No I agree, but we'll take you home.'

Bizarrely this medication – if such it could be called – had driven her to confess things which in a more cold and calculating frame of mind, she would never have dreamt of.

At the end, as she stood up and was clearly dizzy, I put an arm under her right armpit to steady her and took her to await the police surgeon's arrival.

Later, Inspector Sear said with a touch of humour, 'Una, I thought you were a good girl?'

I gave him a puzzled look.

'Three police forces are trying to track you down.'

He passed over an email. I had abducted one Amanda Fairless from a rehab centre in Carlisle and – it was assumed – then taken her to work in an unidentified brothel.

I explained that she was the sister of my ex-boyfriend, had left of her own free will and was now working with the catering staff on a cruise ship.

He smiled. 'I'll ring the shipping line to confirm and ensure that everything tallies – which I've no doubt it will – and then contact this oppo in Carlisle to close the matter.'

My conjecture was that the rehab staff had stirred up this drama simply to brighten up their own dreary lives or make themselves feel important.

On Saturday, I awoke to hear a lark chirping, its monotone notes interspersed with trills. I decided to drive up to Newcastle.

Sophie and I were pleased to see one another, even though our paths had now diverged temporarily. She seemed even dafter than usual.

'I'm managing the Greek, much to my tutor's surprise.'

'And the Old Gaelic and the Etruscan?'

'Very funny.' Her other two blocks were early history stuff. She pummelled me playfully.

We walked to the coffee-shop in Acorn Road.

'Do you think I could be an actress, too?' she asked in mock earnest.

'I thought you were one?'

'I was in a play at school, *The Sleep of Kings*. I was a ghost ... and I think I was all right.'

'Yes, well that sort of fits doesn't it?'

She just laughed.

I had a sense that she was holding something back, but such seemed to be the staple stuff with Sophie dialogues.

'I took the Metro out to Tynemouth on the off-chance ... and saw Osric.'

'That was incredibly good of you.'

'I said you "might come up" and would certainly ask after him.'

'And is he still "shacked-up" with this physio-terrorist?'

'Yes. He's not happy though. I could tell. I told him my best joke and he didn't even smile.'

'That's no surprise.'

I took a second drubbing, but nearly cried as I thought of him. I knew already that I would forgive him.

'I said he ought not to envy you your advantages, but just to be grateful, *very* grateful, that you were devoted to him and loved him.'

'And how did he respond?'

'He didn't really. By the way, Sibylle's thrown in the towel.'

'Oh. So no more quandaries about which professor to charm?'

'Or which one to goose-step after on the ward?' She folded over in silent laughter.

'Or which one will sign her off as "permitted to charge fees"?' I told Sophie of my night with Keith.

'Well, as a one-off I don't think it matters … as long as it doesn't become a habit.' She grinned. 'Tempting though it is?'

'No. I know.'

We finished our cappuccini and panini, hugged one another and parted.

Afterwards I wondered why I had not asked her if she were in love? She had seemed so manic, so vibrant.

In Gateshead I posted the sixteen envelopes I

had brought with me. It would not need an expert graphologist to prove that Fraser had written that letter to Sibylle.

Soon afterwards, I popped home again and told Mummy of Sophie's visit to Osric and of her opinion that he was unhappy.

Daddy was away at a synod meeting.

She cuddled me. 'Go and see him, dear. Don't let pride stop you. At least then you'll have done what you feel is right. What he then does ... well, that's on his shoulders.'

Mummy and I sat on the sofa, since the episode of *Duff Bluff* with me in it was on that evening at ten-fifteen. I keeled over onto her lap and watched it sideways on. She stroked my hair and rubbed my tummy, whilst I drew up my knees and held her free hand in mine.

'They altered the dialogue so much that the script-writer asked for her name to be removed.'

In a Swedish airport, I approached a man eating salted pigs' ribs and mashed turnip.

'Excuse me, but I'm looking for a Mr Dyer?'

'Dyer 'ere. And you are?'

'Dinah, the explosives' contact.'

'So Dinah might it ... '

I said to Mummy, 'You can see why Alison wanted her name erased from the credits.'

I ordered bangers and smash and showed him a note. 'One line's been added in ... hand-written.'

'Ah, the *pen*-ultimate line?'

If spies could pun this badly, the country was in danger.

A critique of this dramatisation had called it a 'masterpiece of espionage humour', but I felt it was the critique itself which was the 'masterpiece of humour'.

In bed, I whispered to Lucy, 'I cannot be with anyone else.' I kissed her. 'I shall just do other things and wait and hope ... My faith in the rightness of being with him is so total, Lucy ... so infinite ... as true as the universe which encompasses us.' I wept silently. 'And I know ... I know for sure that he too is fighting a battle in himself.'

I awoke from a dream. Our railway station had been beautifully restored. Osric had been counting out coins onto a chequer-board whilst I had sat eating bread and honey. 'And you Lucy, were you the maid, hanging out the clothes?' Or had it been our future daughter, whom I had seen?

CHAPTER TWENTY-TWO

Anthea, our house-cleaner in Sloe Buxcomb, only in her thirties yet unkempt and weary-looking, awoke me to the necessity of recovering some fizz or zest. Her surname looked as if it had been constructed by someone dipping their hand randomly into a Scrabble bag.

A Churchill saw came to me; 'In defeat defiance and in victory magnanimity.' The social services – in whose coiled tentacles I would have become a self-doubting vegetable – had been defeated. Therefore it was perhaps time to relent, to be less antagonistic and more forgiving?

They were to launch a further surprise attack, but I did not know this then.

My true way lay with Osric and the rift could only be bridged by a more lowly, gentle and sympathetic Mary.

Genesis says: 'Your servant is unworthy of all the true and steadfast love which has been shown to her.'

Working with the police, you learn to be more observant. It is usually evident who is bad, who is neutral and – alas more rarely – who is good. Superintendent Drake had said, 'We try to look for redeeming features ... if there are any.'

And so in early April, I drove to Tynemouth. It was a dry evening and I hid behind a clump of bushes in front of a boarded-up Victorian villa on the opposite side of the road to Osric's flat.

Lights were on and as dusk fell, a figure – a girl by her outline – closed the curtains behind the French windows.

I had said to Inspector Sear that surveillance must require a lot of patience, to which he had replied, 'It does, but if you catch someone or see something, it is very satisfying.'

A second hour had slipped by, when the main door of Como House opened and a rather short girl appeared with Osric behind her. She turned round, held his face between her hands and kissed it, before crossing the road and passing within ten feet of my hidey-hole. Her hair was short, her neck short, her breasts huge and her bottom wide and flabby. She climbed into an orange soft-top Volkswagen Beetle and drove off rather jerkily.

So busty Angie was no myth, though she had seemingly not been chosen for her looks – boobs excepted – so some comfort there.

I walked swiftly to my pale yellow Panda and drove quickly off, also turning right into Hotspur Street as she had. I spotted her car in one of the parking slots in the centre of Front Street.

I found her not in *The Fruitless Precaution*, but in *The Runaway*.

I ordered a curved yellow cornucopia-like glass of chocolate ice-cream with purple-coloured berries and a coffee.

I watched discreetly as she titivated her make-up using a pocket mirror and an eye-liner brush. Her face was pale but blotchy, for she had rampant acne.

I dug into my ice-cream. The bond tying Osric and myself did not have its source in any human will. He wished to deny the undeniable, to dispel the undismissible. I did not need to cajole or beg. The angels were with me ... so long as I sustained my humility.

On the journey up, I had deliberately subdued any sparks of anger, any whiff of hurt. Grief or sorrow – but not self-pity – were more likely to win this battle.

Angie was joined by a girlfriend. Both were rigged up in tarty night-clubby clothes and numerous bangles and after coffees and giggles, they left.

I drove cautiously after them, keeping a couple of cars between us and so remained unnoticed. Her use of the rear-view mirror would in any case I guessed, be minimal.

In Whitley Bay, under a horse-shoe of gaudy flashing lights, they entered a club, *The Nockstone*.

I bought a ticket, a touch self-consciously since my everyday clothes and lack of make-up would make me stand out. As my eyes adjusted to the gloom, I saw in the stroboscopic flashes of red and purple, the frozen outlines of girls dancing. They were killing time perhaps, whilst waiting for the more piquant 'it' to occur.

The music – by Quince and the Haystacks – had deep regular bass chords, two of them which alternated now and then.

Some guy offered me a bottle with a straw in it.

'No thanks.' I was not going to touch anything here.

'Do you have a boyfriend?'

'Yes,' I said forcefully.

He moved closer so I moved away.

He eyed the little gold cross hung round my neck and leered. 'Are you one of those deluded Christians?'

'Yes.'

'We had a teacher who tried to interpret the Scriptures for us ... a load of poppycock.'

'There's an old proverb; "The Bible is its own interpreter."'

He gave a short laugh, with a hint of a sneer about it and wandered off.

I stood alone for a time and watched the activity in this thinly inhabited dark cavern. Loose behaviour although eye-catching, is neither appealing nor 'cool'.

A girl drifted up to me, smirking but not in an unfriendly way. 'Ralph says you're religious?'

'Yes, that's true.'

'What's the point? What does prayer do?'

'What's your name?'

'Charlie.'

'Well Charlie, it is true that prayer will not change God, but it will change the one who prays.' I had quoted Kierkegaard.

She smiled and walked away as if she had met a green-headed Martian.

Then I spotted Angie snogging furiously with Ralph, exchanging wet smackers and fumbling his bits none too discreetly with her hand down his trousers. Did ninety per cent of their nerves terminate with their genitalia?

I left and set off for Evesham, but on nearing the Tyne Tunnel was stopped by a police car with a blue light.

The officer's pullover had two pips on each epaulette.

'Good evening, Inspector.'

'Good evening,' he smiled. 'Mary Fleet?'

'Yes.'

'Mary, I do not know why you visited *The Nockstone*, but please be careful.'

'Oh?'

'If the junkies there discover that you work for the police, they may decide that you're an *agent provocateur* ... and harm you.'

'I had not thought of that, but thank you.'

He gave me a kindly nod.

At home, I baked a cake; an hour of preparation for a moment of succulence perhaps? I wished I could do the same for a meeting with Osric. I would be more gentle with him in future, because now I understood that he too had glacé cherries and a delicate marzipan coating, which I had not seen before.

Tynemouth again or not?

I used to be very stubborn. When small Mummy had taken me to the doctor's for some mild fever. He had asked, 'You're not suffering from headaches, are you?'

'Yes, sometimes, in the evenings.'

'Yes, but only short ones which soon go?'

'Well no. Sometimes they last for a few hours.'

Many would have submitted and allowed him to settle on his intended diagnosis.

Girls can be extremely blinkered when it comes to men who charm or flatter, but also to the more insidious harm done by their own lack of kindness. Men have strange blind spots too of course, whole galaxies of them.

'My poor lost sparrow, you need love and succour.' A world that had seemed so easily within reach, had slipped away ... but not forever. It lingered there, waiting for us, just over the horizon. I had faith; infinite faith.

Sophie rang, asking to come and see me in the Cotswolds, with her 'new friend'.

'Your new friend?'

'Yes, you had a visitor ... but not Osric this time.'

'Then who?'

'All will become clear, dear. Be patient.'

She could be so annoying.

'Do you remember Gisela, who shares a flat with Kevin and Yvonne?'

'Yes.'

'She said to tell you that Mandy has become engaged to a French steward. They're living near Harwich and she's the office junior at a brick works.'

I was lost for words. What a miraculous outcome?

My next-door neighbour, Hermione Locke, was a police constable.

I knew the constables least of all, because except for being in the parade room at change-over or in the charge room if they had brought someone in, they were usually out on the beat.

'Just a social call,' she said, 'to ask if you're settled in?'

'I've some left-over cake which I baked, so come in.' I smiled, after all I did not have much company.

She played football, was keen on horse-riding and quite athletic in her build, but not pretty.

'Any fun on the beat today?'

She pondered this. 'Beat 2E. Some fellow climbing over the spiked railings at Parry's claimed the wind had blown his cap over them.'

'And you said?'

'I looked a touch sceptical and suggested he go round to the man on the main gate.'

She swayed her sinewy body on the tall breakfast chair.

'Tuesday night was more fun. We chased some joy-riders in a Mini which rolled right over and then carried on with no windows and the roof partly squashed down.'

'Like a mobile observation bunker?'

'We stopped it in Lower Stanton with a stinger ... one of those spiky tyre-deflating scissor things.'

She had longish red hair pulled back into a bun and pale skin with a smattering of freckles. Her manner though lacked openness or warmth and I did not take to her.

She mentioned the site of a medieval battle nearby, where Simon de Montfort had met his end.

'I found a funny bit of corroded bronze there, apparently called a "caltrop". It had four spikes all angled at one hundred and twenty degrees to one another, so when you threw it down it would land on three and leave the fourth one sticking up ... an anti-cavalry device. They were sown in a field where they thought there might be a charge ... and if the spike stuck in the soft part of a horse's hoof it would bolt and throw its rider.'

I nodded slowly.

'Have you ever ridden?'

'Once. A half-Arab and it threw me off ... but it wasn't a caltrop.'

She smiled. 'When a horse is trotting, the rhythm of the pommel can be pleasantly stimulating to our girly parts.'

'Oh?' I would hesitate to discuss such even with Sophie, let alone with a complete stranger. Then I remembered the talk about psychopaths; 'They will be trying to steer the conversation to some objective.'

'Are your eyes yellow or hazel? They're a little unusual?'

'Not especially so.' I felt a touch uneasy and did not refill our coffee cups. She was rapidly wearing out her welcome.

Undaunted, she changed her sitting position. 'Women are more alert I think to bodily movements, whilst men talk about aeroplanes or motorbikes or the sex act.'

I said nothing.

She sighed. 'You're amazingly pretty, Una.'

I thought of refashioning her nose, since it was a bit twisted, but decided that any new deformity could only be an improvement. Besides she looked a lot stronger than I.

'Men like pretty girls ... but also ... '

'Look, if you don't mind, I think you should leave.'

'You don't understand, do you?'

'Yes, I think I do *actually*.'

'I'm a Lesbian. Don't you have any feelings like that? We don't need *men*,' she ended with distaste.

'Look, just go.'

The tiny back garden of my little rented house, fenced with solid creosoted vertical boards, consisted of rough grass with a single border of blue phlox mixed with weeds.

One Saturday, in the midday sunshine, I sat in the basket chair suspended from a steel frame which with its cushions was so comfy. I sat rocking myself by occasionally pushing against the small wooden table with my feet. A bee busied itself rolling in nectar nearby and feeling sleepy, I put down my bowl of cereal and the *A Surfeit of Devils* script.

I dreamt that I drank coffee in the Acorn Road coffee-shop in Jesmond. Osric was there and as he turned from the counter and saw me, he jumped so violently that a half of his coffee ended up in the saucer. He just stood and stared, then slowly sat down.

'May I join you?'

'Of course.'

'Mary ... I'm so, so sorry. I am not living a right life ... I just know it. I am meant to be with you.'

'Yes. I know ... I know.'

Our four hands came together in the middle of the table and I felt the impossibility that we should not coalesce once again.

He had tried to resist my pull, to cling to this other girl, but however hard he tried it could never be right. I felt sorry for him, patient and willing to wait and forgive for what is false must fall apart, must crumble.

The dying rattle of a sports car's engine woke me and heralded visitors at my back gate.

'Mary Fleet?'

'Yes?'

'Nicki Riding. Private detective. Would you mind if we spoke with you?'

'What about?'

'Social Services ... libellous photos?'

Such encounters are two-edged swords; on the plus side, you might learn something; on the minus side, you risk making a slip.

My short navy skirt had ridden up so that my white panties were visible. I stood up and straightened it out.

'Algy Chavasse,' said the fellow in his thirties. 'We rang the bell, but no one's in the house I take it?'

Mary of Magdala whispered, 'Beware. These are devils, barbed and from the redder ends of their spectra.'

'Bring those two old chairs over and sit down.'

The young woman produced a driving licence. 'Nicki Riding' could have been a stage name, invented for its sexual connotations or its *je ne sais quoi*.

'Muesli?' she grimaced. 'What's its fat content?'

'I haven't a clue.'

'We're based in Andoversford. A mere stone's throw away,' observed Algy.

If you were Heracles.

Nicki wore a skimpy red dress and Algy a pink shirt; jelly and blancmange at children's parties came to mind.

'We've just had a ploughman's at *The Puff and Puffer* in Broadway ... Broadway just down the road that is, not Broadway in New York.'

'Oh.'

Algy brushed some hair out of his face and coughed. 'Before David Fraser had his accident, his house was burgled?'

'Yes. So the police have told me.'

'The Northern Social Services wish to limit the spread of some libellous photos and papers which were stolen.'

'Oh.'

'We're here to represent them and to negotiate a settlement with you.'

'Forgive me, I'm lost?'

'You possess these items, we believe?'

'Then you're misinformed.'

'It's a political hot potato so far as they're concerned.'

'Political? It's a binary question. Either I have the documents or I don't.'

Nicki ignored this. 'Mary, a financial solution is on offer.'

Algy surveyed my thighs closely, half-visible below my plain cotton skirt.

'My surname's Anglo-Norman,' Algy said. 'My ancestors came over with William the Conqueror. I was educated at Sherborne and my paternal grandfather was a wealthy colonial tea-planter, but the world is changing … and we have to adapt.'

'Adapt?'

'Make money some other way.'

I eyed a wasp buzzing above the fence. 'Oh. Are you an advocate of *les folies de grandeur*?' I asked drily.

They looked puzzled.

'You're suggesting bribery?'

'Yes.' Nicki gave a sweetly sarcastic grin.

'Not everyone whores after money.'

'Do you think it wrong then, to be ambitious?'

'Not if it's done honestly and without harming others … but I don't have these papers anyway.'

The wasp stung Nicki's left breast.

Her dress had a deep frontal split which exposed the inner segments of her breasts. A segment is the area bounded by a part of a circle's circumference and a chord, if I recall my school geometry lessons rightly?

'Ouch.' She gave a yelp, then used the f-word.

'Oh Nicki, you're so unlucky lately. Pipped at the post twice with interviews … '

'I'm allergic to bees and wasps.' She inspected the wound area which had already become coin-sized and red.

'I've been "leap-frogged" too,' admitted Algy. Modern life is so tough.'

'Oh.'

'They say you can drop a glass ten times and nothing happens, but then the eleventh time it smashes.'

'Oh?'

He was almost ranting. 'Conspiracy theories – that others are behind the Fraser burglary – do not hold up. Just be sensible Mary and think of a figure they might accept in return for your signature?'

Nicki's whole breast was becoming swollen and purple.

She started to feel faint, to show signs of shock. We laid her down on the grass, put her feet up on a chair and rang 999.

I thought of Hezekiah on the ramparts of Jerusalem as the besieging Assyrian army began to perish. This wasp sting, if not yet excellent, was at least promising. As Algy knelt down beside her, I discreetly slipped Nicki's shoulder bag behind the dustbin.

To counter the widespread dilatation of her veins, the ambulancemen jabbed some adrenaline under her skin, put up a drip, squeezed it, then took her away.

I took some photographs.

Out on the road, Algy in quite a fury, sneered at my thirteen-year-old Panda. 'Are you happy with this crap? Does it go?'

I patted her on the roof and whispered, 'Don't worry. I love you.'

Were they on commission? No deal, no fee?

An ear-piercing screech followed as a builder's lorry roared by, scraping the side of Algy's sports car before vanishing in a cloud of dust.

The raging blancmange leapt in and gave chase.

I felt quite undaunted by these mediocre envoys, just as Jeremiah had faced his arch-enemies, the false priests and unseeing soothsayers, in Jerusalem.

I drove to a disused chalk quarry, where I opened Nicki's bag. I switched off the voice-recorder, put it inside a plastic bag and hammered it to pieces with a rock. Some papers gave her an alternative name, Tatiana Dubovna. I bashed her mobile phone between rocks, cut up her bank cards and pocketed a substantial wad of money. At the household waste tip I dumped it all – except for the money – in a well-knotted plastic bag.

At home, I drank tea and then knelt to uproot some weeds from between the gentian-coloured phlox; a simple but soothing task.

Algy reappeared. 'She arrested just as she arrived at the hospital in Worcester. They resuscitated her, but say she may have suffered heart and brain damage.'

I showed no sympathy.

'Where's her bag?'

'Bag? I haven't a clue.'

He glowered. 'Oh yes you have ... bloody Mary.'

I stood firm. 'Don't you dare touch me.'

Back on Tyneside the next day – a Sunday – I went to Como House, but no one was in.

In Jesmond, neither was Sophie. Adrian thought she had gone to Edinburgh.

'Edinburgh? Why has she gone there? And her phone's off.'

He gave me tea and we spoke of our common enemy. I mentioned the Bill Mead case – without giving names – and said how it had ended in their buying him off with a huge lump of compensation. 'But no one was sacked or disciplined, yet the chief executive and a couple of others should have ended up in the slammer.'

'They talk "ethics" whilst having no ethics and think only of the retention of power.'

'Still it's par for the course for these shockers. The oceans of money wasted on this "care" circus?'

I said that I was on my way to see Osric with the hope of mending our fences.

'I had a girlfriend where things went pear-shaped and it seemed that it was my fault, but – on reflection – I think I was reacting to her selfishness.'

'How do you mean?'

'She wanted everything her way and eventually I started to resist.'

'Oh?'

In Newcastle, I bought Osric a pair of below-knee navy breeches and a blue and white T-shirt with a shattered frothy artistic pattern on it. It reminded me of Hokusai's 'The Great Wave of Kanagawa'.

So, off to Tynemouth. I thought of 'Fling wide your gates.' Mine were open; my portcullis drawn up.

I rang his bell and he answered, as I had known he would.

I smiled brightly. 'Hullo Osric.'

'Er ... hullo.'

He tried to look away or take a step backwards, but was unable to do so.

I suddenly burst into uncontrollable sobs.

He stood frozen for a moment, then asked, 'Do you want to come in.'

I nodded jerkily and tried to dry my tears. Inside I said, 'I so want to be back with you.' He was unshaven. I handed him the clothes. 'A parcel for Mr Bristle.'

He took hold of me. Perhaps my need, my weakness, finally gave him more confidence. The sun did not revolve only around me.

For almost an hour we sat and just held one another. Finally I spoke, my voice turning into a squeak. 'Shall we have a boiled egg?'

'Yes. That would be nice.' He looked distraught. 'Mary I know I've done wrong ... I can't live without you ... my mind fills up with hideous thoughts and I can't prevent it.'

'No matter. We're going to be together again now.'

'You are so pure and I am not.'

'No, that is not true, but ... and it's not that simple Osric.'

The egg-yolk was orange, not yellow.

Although it appeared that I was his saviour, this act of love and forgiveness was also my own salvation.

'King David, even when he did bad deeds, God forgave him and set him on the right way again. He crushed his enemies and saved him from all kinds of mishap.'

'He was big enough to admit his faults?'

'But if you wish to do wrong, then God's all-knowing

watchfulness is an unwelcome intrusion.'

He looked so serious that I both laughed and cried. Tears dripped onto the plate around my egg.

I guessed that one day we would marry, but perhaps this was my wedding day?

CHAPTER TWENTY-THREE

Mary could have spent her life in Magdala or another of the villages on the shore of Lake Galilee. By the well or at the market, she would have heard the old women grumble about their aches and ailments or the young ones whisper of Hannah having to marry that likely-lad goat-herd Zebadiah. At home she would have swept the floor and baked the bread.

Yet had perhaps a royal entourage halted on the road, where a courtier or a cup-bearer, spotting her artless beauty, had offered her a post as a maid at court? Her father – persuaded to give his consent by a handful of shiny gold aurei – had then permitted his young, shy, astute daughter to taste the dubious splendours of palace life. Its vulgar extravagance and exoticism had though drawn her gradually down into a state of fear and darkness, shadows from which release had only come through contrition and forgiveness.

Sergeant Hines was on duty at the desk. His boots were off and his feet rested on a second chair, whilst he nursed a large mug of tea.

Hines was a soul at peace with itself, in no hurry to tell you how amazing he was. He had a very strange and awkward girlfriend named Deirdre, who had bought a canal boat named *Lily*. 'There's a lot wrong with her, but I should be able to fix most of it.'

'What the boat or Deirdre?'

He managed a smile, just. 'That was a bit cheeky, Miss Una.'

Hermione entered in civvies. 'I'm in to catch up on some report-writing, Sergeant,' she said in a prickly tone, then seeing me added, 'Oh Una, there's a report on a builder's lorry taking the side off a sports car and not stopping, which I believe you witnessed?'

'I'll come and tell you what I know.'

Hines asked about a brawl on Waterside.

'We all went down in the van.' Hermione smiled more brightly. 'It was quite a lark. I had my foot on some guy's neck till Sergeant Sladden told me to ease off.'

'Sergeant Sladden was in charge? That's what I wanted to know.'

She waltzed off with a stiff gait.

'She has a hard shell,' murmured Hines. 'She's sampling a cohabitation with a beauty therapist, to see if they're "compatible". Her trouble though is an inability – or an unwillingness – to love.'

In the spare office, sat with her sea of forms, Hermione gave me a smile. 'I'm seeing a boy on Friday.'

'Oh. Good. Good luck.'

'I don't want to have sex on a first date though, especially with a boy ... I would feel low.'

'Well, just go out for a coffee, hold hands ... tell him to cool down if he's too pushy ... and try to be kind to him.'

'Oh?'

These folk just live in another cosmos.

Later Chloë rang to say she had just come back from Moscow; V.I.P treatment, dinner in the Kremlin. 'Then, when Graham needed to get home quickly for an important vote in the House, we had a blue-light escort to the airport.'

I could hear Offenbach tinkling in the background.

'Zoë's very confident about Angus Robertson. He's only thirty-one, but she senses that we're in competent hands.'

'That's encouraging.'

'And Graham has found two definite sponsors for the film.'

The plot of *A Surfeit of Devils* revolved around three archetypal or caricatured German aristocrats, who wished to have their evil way with three actresses – French, English and Russian – but are outwitted and tricked out of a castle, a fortune and some art works.

I wondered if a line from Fraser's Sibylle letter might be reconfigured and uttered by the base Graf Dieter von Klunk. 'Actresses are not as pure and radiant as they like to pretend on stage.'

I collected Sophie from the station.

'You can swing in my comfy garden chair.'

'You look happy again. Are we no longer pining for Osric?'

'We're together again.'

She looked surprised.

'It's so wonderful. I finish here in August, then back to Newcastle. We should both qualify next summer. Anyway, your new boyfriend?'

'He's coming up from Bath and should be here soon.'

Angus Robertson arrived, a trifle austere but with a certain presence. Much that he said – apart from its obvious meaning – carried unstated implications for you to unravel. This freedom from excess is one of the more attractive attributes of the Scots.

'So you're to be our producer ... and you're with Sophie?'

'He came to Otterburn Terrace looking for you.'

'And you gave him tea?'

'Previously I had believed that men were never "just passing", but this time it was true.'

I smiled.

'I've given her a small part as a sorceress,' he said. 'It seemed apt.'

He struck me as open and dependable. If you had to trust someone, he would be a sensible gamble.

My bones were telling me that *A Surfeit of Devils* would succeed.

Angus started to light his pipe. He focused on the flame until after a series of short sharp puffs, the tobacco ignited. 'I hear you have a subsidiary *rôle* coming up Mary, in *Cold Iron*?'

'I'm in three short scenes.'

'And the plot?'

'A girl attempts to use the darker arts to draw a boy's affections away from his true love.'

'Very simple then ... in its basic theme?'

They set off for Newcastle and four days later, having a week's leave, I set off too.

Osric and I went to our railway station. The container was rusting and the weeds were flourishing and flowering.

We sat on one of the wide brick gate-posts with our arms around each other's waists and were silent. Yet one day ... we would live here.

Claude drove the 1937 Albion out to Mr Marshall, an old anvil and some milk churns strapped onto its flat cargo deck. He and Osric wore baggy flannels, chequered waistcoats and caps and I a capacious calf-length dress of striped dimity and a broad hat with a wide ribbon tied under my chin. We were half-way to a Gilbert and Sullivan operetta. The lorry had been painted scarlet with black mudguards – four coats of paint and two of varnish – and the lettering was in gold with black shadowing; 'K BONSALL LTD.' At an outdoor buffet, we drank champagne and ate raspberries and clotted cream off a trestle-table, with bunting rigged up above us. Her new owner said that she had already been booked for a part in a film.

In Sloe Buxcomb, in the pub, my old school friend Josh told of his falling in love in Cardiff.

'When I saw her I could not think of anything to say. Silly banter is easy when you have no deep feelings, but when you're in love you grow all solemn and tongue-tied and sound like a half-wit.'

'You're actually more entertaining when you're not trying to be,' said Sarah.

Josh looked unsure how to take this.

Emily had fallen in love, but her boy had left her to work in Iceland. She had married someone else, but left him in less than a year. 'Then she met her first love again and now they live in Brixham, where she's an assistant in a chemist's ... and I think very happy.'

Love is not such a bundle of vagaries.

An anonymous letter claimed that the senior ward sister in Newcastle – one Debra Hammersley – had received a four figure sum to retract her statement. The local authority's treasurer had requested that a forensic accountant be engaged to trace various unexplained and anonymised payments, but had been overruled by the chief executive.

Jill Vickerton took early retirement, with an enhanced pension, naturally. This foiled any awkward inquiries. As the psalmist says though, 'No one can ransom a soul.'

I said to Osric, 'If Sharon just took a job in a supermarket, her life would improve by a thousand per cent. How can we fix that?'

'She needs a change of attitude.'

Daddy and Osric went off to an air show to see a restored Westland *Lysander*.

I ironed some of his surplices and albs and took them over to the vestry.

A painting hung there of the Reverend Hector Collett, dated 1741. After dining at the squire's one winter's evening – and drinking too much claret – he had collapsed in the lane whilst walking home. Some miners on their way to the night-shift found him. They could not leave him there to freeze nor not go to work, so they took him with them. The mine had two shafts. A fire at the bottom of one created an up-draught so causing the air to circulate. The story is that he woke up terrified, in this black cavern beside this huge brazier where he had been left to thaw out.

I sat on an old semi-circular oaken chair and gazed at him.

For the paints used by the Renaissance artists, mineral and plant dyes had been brought from far afield, on camels say even from as far away as Uzbekistan. It required skill to produce these basic colours of which there were only ten or twelve. Why such an effort? Was it just rivalry between the various Italian towns for beauty and adornment or a wish that we might be ennobled by their subjects?

I thought once again of Goethe: 'There is no noble

crown – well-worn or ill-worn – which is not a crown of thorns.'

I cried, but happily. Only truth is liberating and though ultimately incomprehensible, the search for it is in essence a form of love. Totalitarianism in any guise is the foe – Paris kidnapping Helen – for wisdom is displayed in the simplicity of her delights and the lightness of her heart.

'Mary of Magdala, pattern and symbol of struggle, guide and watch over me in the coming years.'

THE END.